BLESSING

BRIAN J. TWIDDY

Tapping Frog Literary Ltd
5 Glenalmond House, London, SW15 3LP

www.tappingfrog.com

First published in 2023 by Tapping Frog Literary

A catalogue record for this book is available from the British Library

Paperback ISBN: 978-1-916647-00-8
eBook ISBN: 978-1-916647-01-5

This novel is entirely a work of fiction. The names, characters, and incidents portrayed in it are the work of the author's imagination. Any resemblance to actual persons, living or dead, events or localities is entirely coincidental.

Typeset by Tapping Frog Literary

Printed and bound by CPI Group (UK) Ltd, Croydon, CR0 4YY

"There is a crowd behind me, lifting me to the light.
They carry me forward, from thence comes my might."

— BEN SAPHAN

Through their patience, hard work and encouragement, my
crowd include my beautiful wife Yvonne and the kids, the ever
supportive Annarie and Simon, and not least Ed, Flo, Tess,
Toby, Becca, Charlotte et al in the writer's room.

Thank you all.

THE BOOK OF DEVON

This is a hell of a town. I love it. Wouldn't want to live any place else. Never have. That is leastways since I was about ten years old. That was when we got here, in 1982, in the back of Uncle Lucas' car.

It was lucky we weren't stopped, or crashed into, the way he drives. There were cries of 'Slow down Lucas' and 'Mind them bumps' from my mother, whose overly large frame was taking up most of the back seat, leaving what little remained to be shared by myself and another lady with her kid. I didn't know, at the time, who they were, but she kept saying 'Small up yoursel', behave Adey' and 'Be quiet, Adey boy' as Uncle Lucas drove as fast as he could, and all over the road.

'Stop your yammering Lucas and watch the road' made no difference to him. Almost as if he didn't hear her. 'Look where we goin'.' She was almost pleading.

He couldn't seem to stop talking and had to look you right in the eye to make his point.

'This car ain't goin' a make it anywhere further, not like this,' she tried again. It fell on deaf ears, he had rarely been known to listen to anybody anyway, but in this case mainly because of the constant scraping noises.

I could see the road through where the door didn't fit the frame properly and there was a rope of elastic holding the gear stick in place. I don't think he'd ever heard of an MOT. Come to that, neither had I, but why would I, I was ten.

He'd picked us up from the small boat after dark. The people we had crossed with had disappeared very quickly in all directions, except for Adey and his mother, and it was all very much of a scramble.

'Mummy, it's been hours, I'm hungry.' I was on the verge of crying.

'Not long now darlin', we're nearly there and then we'll have a good ol' cook up,' she said trying to be soothing.

'You young uns ain't got the fortitude we had when we was kids, we was hungry and tired, mos' of the time, and complaining don't change nothin'. I remember one time, oh years back now, me and your dad, well we couldn't have been much older 'n you are now…".

I didn't listen much to Uncle Lucas. It just all sounded the same anyway, in one long stream of words. I was busy trying to peer through the dirty windows at the brightly lit streets that we were flying through.

'Wind up the windows, I'm gettin' cold,' said my mum as she pulled her coat tighter. She really felt the cold too. I don't think the car could have had a heater. Though to be fair, it shouldn't have needed one, as we were all crammed in so tight our body heat alone should have kept us warm. The problem was that the windows were steaming up so much on the inside, that even the dirt on the outside was blurry, and Uncle couldn't see the road.

'If I wind 'em up I can't see nuthin',' said Uncle, turning in his seat, followed immediately by a shriek of 'Watch the road!' So we had to have the windows open.

The shops were different, they were mostly brick, as far as I could make out, and in long rows. Every time we turned there were more, stretching out ahead. The smell was different too.

'Why does it smell, Mummy?' It smelled stale, oniony, the air felt sharp. It made me feel odd. Everything suddenly seemed to be happening to someone else and I forgot where we were, it couldn't have been for long, then the world sort of re-focused.

'Where'd you go Dev, pay attention, look around your new world, everywhere has its own smell, even back home.'

I wondered what she meant.

'Back home?'

'Ah, but it did love, it's just that you got used to it being all around you every day. Here is different is all. After a few days you won't notice it at all.'

The smell did go, but it wasn't because I was used to it. It was to return from time to time, accompanied by the same sensation and usually followed by a short period when the world sort of went away. Then coming back, sometimes, with people shouting at me and telling me I'd 'disappeared' for a while. It was never diagnosed, but the old wives club knew all the answers. At the time it was just 'leave the poor mite be, he's over tired is all.'

Even at that hour of night there were a lot of people about on the street. Shops were still open, and thriving it seemed. The cars, trucks, and motorbikes were all fighting for position on the road, like some never-ending race; even huge buses, with upstairs floors, were competing. The place was alive. Then we turned, and it all disappeared. It just faded behind us. Now the houses were darker, only occasional light escaped them, competing with the dim street lamps for dominance. We turned again and now even the street lamps were gone. The only light was from the headlamps of the car.

Suddenly, 'Here we are. Safe and soun'. Why all the worries eh? Home sweet home,' said Uncle Lucas as we pulled up outside a very dark house, in a seemingly endless row of very dark houses. I can only think that we were hustled out of the car; our few belongings that were on our laps spilled out onto cracked, weedy concrete in front of this particular silhouette. I was pushed along, tripping on the baggage.

I looked up to see a massive shape looming over me. It said it was my dad. It had been so long, I hardly recognised him, particularly in the dark. This giant of a man caught hold of me and picked me up as easily as a bag of yams. As he spun me around I looked behind me, and the car, with its remaining passengers, was already pulling out of the driveway, its twin beams trying to pierce the gloom ahead of it. A booming laugh came from the giant and he dropped me to the ground.

Then it was quiet. So this was England. I wondered if the Queen lived in one of the dark houses. It was later, that I learned that England was the country. The town was London, and the Queen didn't live in a terraced house.

We, as a family, moved around from house to house, to flat, to room, and back again quite frequently; never very far but far enough for it to be considered 'somewhere else'. To a different borough, different school. Mum said not to use our family name, Lawrence, I don't know why, I liked it. We had to be called Lucas after our uncle. Whatever paperwork we needed he always provided, with no explanation but it always had his name. The schools were mostly accommodating, 'Oh, yes we can find a temporary place for you.'

Dad always seemed to be busy, often at night, so I didn't see an awful lot of him, but he always made sure we had a roof, wherever it was, and enough to eat. I never knew how he made a living, but there were good weeks when we had plenty to eat and bad weeks when we went to the market at the end of the day to pick up leftovers. I discovered television. We didn't have one, it would be far too awkward to carry from place to place, never mind the cost but I loved watching other people's, particularly the adverts with the catchy jingles. My favourite at one time was the Ambrosia creamed rice slogan 'Devon knows how they make it so creamy.' I thought they were saying my name, Devin, and I would say it endlessly in perfect imitation of the voice on TV (I thought). I said it so much that friends and family got sick to death of it and started calling me Devon, which stuck.

Mum was the permanent fixture. Whenever we moved, she made sure we had all of the things around us that made a place into a home, even if it did mean sleeping on the sofa. We eventually did get a TV of our own, through Uncle Lucas. It was an abused portable, ex Radio Rentals, one with a wire coat-hanger stuck in the aerial bit that we had to move about each time we turned the dial to change the channel. The picture was always a bit grainy, but it was ours.

Wherever we lived, Mum instantly set the kitchen up to make our 'favourite' meals – out of whatever we had at the time – and she covered it all in spices so that it all tasted exactly the same. 'Here you are, jus' like back home, don't leave any now, better belly buss than good food waste.' Wherever we were, we were surrounded by the smells of home. Oh, and of course there was Adey.

Adey was a couple of years younger than I was and always seemed to be around. He didn't actually belong to anyone, since his mother went – and it was never clear what happened to her – but he moved around the neighbourhood shadows, a couple of nights here, a weekend there. He stayed over at ours quite a lot, wherever we were.

He was alright to hang out with for a while and sort of became everyone's pet. He wasn't quite like other people, though I couldn't say what was different about him. He didn't have a filter to his thoughts, that was one thing, whatever he thought just came straight out of his mouth. He had a loping sort of walk, as though he was trying to duck down all the time. One thing about Adey, that made me squirm just a little, was that he had no concern for animals, and had no compunction about kicking, squashing, or even on one notable occasion, setting them alight and squealing with laughter: Adey seemed to have a fascination for fire. There was a kind of understanding amongst our community that we would look out for him.

I learned to fit in quickly. Just like Dad would say 'Get to know which tree to climb boy,' to get in with the right people, so I didn't find myself becoming isolated and 'different'. I worked hard but my friends didn't want to stay in and do homework, they wanted to have fun, and so I went to have fun with them. I learned a lot that wasn't on the curriculum, but unfortunately not enough that was.

I had to be careful though. It was one thing fitting in, but I had been warned by my dad that I shouldn't get too close to anyone and that I didn't ought to become a part of anything I wasn't certain about; so I hung around the fringes of groups – which, with time, became the feeding stations for the gangs – and passed through my youth almost unnoticed.

I didn't get many 'O' levels, just Business Studies and French. Business studies were what I was most interested in anyway, it meant running my own business and making a fortune. French, because the French mistress was young and looked like Kelly Le Brock – everyone has a weakness and as it turns out, that's mine. The year after I took them, they changed to GCSE's. Who knows, what difference that may or may not have made?

For some reason, I was fascinated by maps. I wanted to know what London looked like, and where it was in the world. I took an atlas from a school once, it was a very dog-eared old volume, but it showed me England, Scotland, Wales, and Northern Ireland – and all the counties and the towns. It said that the warmest place in the UK was the south west: Devon and Cornwall – *who knew Devon was a place?* So I promised myself, that's where I'd live when I got rich.

I had a plan. To get rich I needed a business. It didn't matter what kind, as business men were always rich. I did retain a lot of the business information from school, and tried to make use of it, but with only two qualifications I found it hard to get a start.

I may not have had much money but I did have principles. There were plenty of opportunities offered by 'friends', where I could make a lot of money, quickly, as long as I didn't ask questions; but I turned them all down, they eventually stopped asking and I watched as those friends – wealthy as they were, and dripping with gold – disappeared from our society for lengthy periods of time; then suddenly re-appeared with little to show for it, except perhaps a rudimentary tattoo, and a swagger. Some never came back.

Sometimes I hung out at the 'rec', which was in fact such a wreck that no self respecting, God-fearing person would be seen dead there. Unless, of course, they were seen – dead. The time that that happened, it was an old tramp sleeping on a bench through one bitterly cold night last winter. Apparently somebody thought she needed warming up, so they set fire to her. The police got involved, and all the black kids – if seventeen and eighteen year olds can be called kids – were brought out of the shadows and interviewed, including me. The police didn't spend much time investigating and nobody was ever held to account for it, but locally everyone seemed to think Adey knew something about it. Nobody ever said though.

I tried my hand at various ventures, or as you might call them, get rich quick schemes. I tried to get in on pyramid selling schemes, but soon found that only the first in got any mileage out of that. None of it was going to get me rich. The only financial advantage I gained, was when Dad died and left me a few thousand pounds. That was a surprise, as nobody knew that he'd had any money at all and, as before, I didn't ask questions. 'Don't trust them banks!' Mum told me, 'They take your money and want to know your whole life, before they give it back to you. Keep it close, so you can count it when you want.' I think she meant in a bag in the cupboard or under the mattress, but there were far too many break-ins around us, and stories about people losing everything, to trust in that.

Mum got poorly, shortly after Dad passed away, so there was no money coming in, or very little, and the amount left her by Dad only lasted until the cold weather started to bite. I had moved away by that time and had my own bills to pay, and I never really noticed. She had never been very strong physically and there was always something; 'My ol' heart keeps pokin' me' and 'These legs won' take much more.' She succumbed to the cold the following winter.

It turned out that Uncle Lucas, wasn't a real uncle at all, just a friend of Dad's from the 'old days', and as soon as the money had run out after Dad died, so had he.

Adey reappeared around that time. He had grown a straggly beard by then and was a lot taller, but instantly recognisable by his walk, though now he wore a hoodie almost all the time. He was one of those that disappeared from time to time. He found it difficult finding work, so was always on the lookout for a handout. I didn't have much, but gave him what I could, bought him a takeaway and promised to stay in touch; and I did, I kept an eye out for him and eventually helped him find a bedsit and a job. The job didn't last long, the bedsit did however – he must have been getting money from somewhere – and he somehow survived.

I had been given some advice about money by one of the guys on some pyramid scheme and, having learned one or two things about the reality of life without cash, I put all my inheritance away in one of the new Gordon Brown ISAs, so that it would get some interest – particularly as interest rates were running at about ten percent – and always still be there if I needed it. I tried working in an office but my organising skills weren't great, and I wasn't really interested in filing other peoples' invoices and purchase orders. However, I did need to work and, as time went on, I learned a little more about businesses, offices, and how it all works; it did pay for rent and day to day expenses.

Of course, my courtship skills were first division. I was

never short of company for an evening out. Which is probably why I never really got ahead, financially speaking.

2004 was a momentous year: a space craft landed on Mars, Mark Zuckerberg launched the Facebook, Michael Schumacher won his seventh world championship, and I met Elina.

I was out in town with Adey, one Saturday afternoon. He pictured himself as my wingman, not that I had much trouble finding romance, but he did, and I think he was hoping some magic would rub off on him if he stayed close enough. We'd been hanging out – he was between jobs at the time – we were watching the world go by, sitting on the steps of a statue of some ancient war hero, trying to amuse ourselves striking matches and seeing who could let them burn down the furthest. He'd spotted a beautiful young (Thai?) girl selling flowers from a cart in the square. He didn't need flowers – I didn't think he knew a daisy from a daffodil – but he thought he'd test his skills. He approached the girl, and chatted for a couple of minutes. They were laughing together and I thought he was coping okay. It was a surprise to me when he came back and said 'Nah, she blew me out. Nice though, said it was her birthday.'

'You just don't have a clue man, watch and learn.' I got up and walked over to where she was busying herself watering various blooms. I examined the flowers on her barrow for a few minutes, then, 'Excuse me, I don't know a lot about flowers and that sort of stuff. But I need to get a nice bunch for a beautiful girl. What's your favourite?'

'Does she like colours or scents?'

'I don't know, which says most about love and devotion and that?'

'I've always like Peruvian lilies for that. Those pink ones

there, they are a bit expensive, or maybe some crocus's, or is it crocii? Everybody likes those. My personal favourite are the asters.'

'Which ones are they?' I asked.

'The white ones there at the back. They have a gorgeous scent.'

'Great, could you make me up a bunch with those in, then. Not too big, but nice?'

'Of course. I could do something small for £7.50.'

'Okay,' I paid her with cash. Fortunately I had just enough on me.

'Give me a few minutes, and I'll have them ready for you.' She turned to get on with it, and I walked back to Adey.

'Well,' he asked. 'How'd you get on, what were you talking about?'

'Flowers,' I said. 'And now I'm going back to ask her out.'

He laughed as I walked back to the barrow. 'Come on, give it up, come and have a drink,' he called from the shadow of the statue and motioned to the Wetherspoons in the square. Too late.

'Hi again,' I said.

'Oh, I didn't see where you went. Here they are. What do you think?'

'I think you are the nicest, most beautiful, girl I have ever met.'

She blushed, 'The flowers.'

'They are stunning. My friend,' I pointed over to where Adey was watching, 'my friend told me it was your birthday. So I want you to have them. Take the rest of the day off, and let me walk you home to put them in some water.'

She looked at me puzzled, then smiled. My heart jumped! *Is that how lightning feels?* I think she said something about the barrow and the flowers wilting. All I heard was the 'No!' at the start. Suddenly, I wanted to see her again, more than anything else that I could think of. If, of course, I had been able to think at all.

She must have seen the look of disappointment on my face. 'But if you come back at about six, you can ask again.'

'I'm Dev. See you then.'

'Elina.'

I stepped away, reeling a little still, turned, blew her a very theatrical kiss, and returned to where Adey was leaning against the bollard. My feet didn't seem to touch the ground. I couldn't take my eyes off her and NASA must have been able to see her smile from Mars; it lit up the whole square. The town. My world. I had never felt so good.

Elina and I really hit it off and, after a whirlwind romance, much to my surprise – and Adey's – we got married. Actually, Elina wasn't Thai at all, she was British, with her great grandparents immigrating here from Singapore. I had one or two little difficulties in that area, owing to the lack of documentation when my mother and I first moved here, but it's at times like these that friends like Adey come in very handy. He got me the right history. I don't know how or where from – but Adey had a life in the shadows, and a circle of friends that I knew nothing about – and I didn't ask. So it came about, very conveniently, that I passed all the legal requirements to get married and that, by marrying her, I finally became a legal British citizen.

The wedding took place in the registry office on a crisp but sunny April afternoon. Elina did her own flowers – she was very good – and she looked beautiful. The reception for the new Mr and Mrs Lucas was in the pub across the square. Adey was the best man, although best for what is debatable, and he made a very short, very rude, alcohol fuelled, speech; after which he fell asleep.

I moved into Elina's bedsit with her, officially, the next day – although given the amount of time I was spending there, I may as well have been living there already – and our life together started. She continued to work the flower barrow and I went out every morning, knocking on doors, looking for work. Any work.

Walking back to the small room one cool, summer evening a few months later – after a day trudging the streets sweating – I passed a little run down shop on a side street with a lease available sign. I stopped to have a better look, although I couldn't see a lot.

'It's not in the best location, but it's not bad, and if the rent's low enough, it might be worth having a go at. Two bedroom flat included' it said. I was good with my hands, well, good enough, I thought. *From the outside not much looks like it needs fixing up, a good clean will probably sort it.* I hurried home and told Elina all about it.

She was very enthusiastic, 'Oh, Dev, can we really have a little shop, of our own? Can we afford it?'

'It's got a flat as well. It probably won't be much more than living here,' I told her. Of course I didn't know what kind of flat, in what condition, or anything else about it; but with enthusiasm, and perhaps a little wishful thinking, and crossed fingers, I said, 'It'll be perfect!'

'A flower shop. I've always dreamed of a proper flower shop. Where we can raise our little family.'

'Hey, hang on a bit! One thing at a time.' I wasn't ready for that.

'Only kidding, but soon eh, soon?'

And that was that. We went to the estate agents the very next day and started the process. It took a few weeks, and some help from the bank, but eventually all paperwork obstacles were removed and, with the aid of a little creative thinking, we signed the lease. The deposit took half of my ISA and some more we'd been able to borrow, and we made our plans. I wanted the shop to be a base from which we could build an empire to rival Interflora. Elina wanted a home to have a family. I wanted contacts all over the country to sell to, from wedding receptions to funeral wakes, birthdays, and christenings. I wanted a company that would deliver flowers for any occasion to anywhere at all. I wanted to import flowers from Europe and Africa, South America, and India; for my team of employees to make up into bouquets or wreaths as necessary. So when we moved into the flat above the little shop, I could see 'The Future', and it was shining bright.

In terms of work needed to get started, there were no real surprises; it was much as I'd thought, a lot of elbow grease, but no major problems. We could start our very own business with perhaps a surface renovation, and a deep clean. I managed with some 'help' from Adey, as long as some money changed hands. He did most of the fetching and carrying necessary – and managed to 'get' one or two difficult items for the window display – and before we knew it, we were ready. We weren't permitted to make any alterations by the terms of the lease, so it was lucky they weren't necessary and lots of paint in lots of colours made up for any shortcomings. We called it Lucas's Lupins. It could have been Lucas's Lilacs, Lilies or even Lotus's, but Elina liked Lupins and I love alliteration.

While Adey helped with the clean up and I repurposed the old shop fittings, Elina looked for suppliers, and started planning the furnishings for the flat; which turned out to be a very nicely arranged two bedroom place, and very habitable. I started looking for customers. The telephone line was connected and I was constantly on it, as well as working in the shop.

Elina had to be up and out early to catch the markets. She came back for a late breakfast and then it was all hands on. Time seemed to be a very precious commodity. A trickle of orders started coming in. To increase those orders – and to 'move the business forward,' I told her – I decided to go on the road, locally anyway, to hotels, churches, any venue that might need flowers. Business was slow at first; I picked up a few small orders from a local hotel and a couple of offices, and that, with meagre earnings from walk in customers, kept us afloat.

The area that I visited got wider; searching for new customers is never easy. It came to a point where I was spending most of my time travelling around and with the occasional night away, due to the onset of an 'episode', had to leave Elina to cope in the shop. She was dealing with it all, and I suppose, no matter how good she was, or how much she loved doing it, she was only one person. When the first big wedding order came in, she was overwhelmed. I mean to say, how she managed was nothing short of a miracle; the hours and hours of hard work that she put into the planning of the church flowers, the bride's bouquet, table dressing for the reception, and boutonnieres for the groom, best man and close relatives, would have finished a lesser woman. She promised herself that she would never be put in that situation again. If I was as successful as we hoped, then these big orders would become more and more frequent, if not the norm. The way things were, although hoping for more business and wanting to be ready to cope with it, the finances weren't yet in a state capable of employing anyone full time; so the only option available was to find someone willing to work part-time, but able to put in extra hours when necessary. So Elina put a card in the shop window, and into the window of the newsagents along the street. It was free for the first week, and a pound per week after that.

That was how Elina met Dot. To give her full name, she was Dorothea Taylor-Wilson. Dot, she had insisted on being called Dot, was a middle-aged, well dressed, woman; fairly tall, slim and with short mouse coloured hair, which one only really got a glimpse of indoors as she habitually wore the most godawful hats I'd ever seen in my life. She had applied almost immediately after Elina's card had appeared. They got on straight away and she was taken on in an instant, solving Elina's pressing staffing problem and saving her at least a pound in fees to the newsagent.

Dot loved flowers, she loved people, and she loved to talk. She had been spending most of her time at home looking after her father – in his mid eighties and suffering from the onset of dementia – so conversation was sadly lacking there and rather repetitive; she often said 'It's like living on a verbal carousel.' Ironic really. Dot wanted company, and a distraction. She had left a long held position as a manager in a mid-sized manufacturing company when she was forced to retire, and her skills very quickly proved themselves of great help to Elina in, not only the day to day working with the flowers, but also organising the business to be much more easily managed as it, hope-fully, grew.

So on Tuesdays, and Thursday afternoons, when the home help carers came to look after her father's needs, Dot was free to help Elina in whatever capacity was required; and during the quieter moments, spend time chatting over a nice cup of tea.

Now that Elina had help, at least on Tuesdays and Thursday afternoons – Dot had organised carers for Mondays too, but insisted on having those days to go and 'breathe the air' as she put it – the work and organisation of Elina's time became easier, and she was less concerned about the time that I spent away drumming up business. It was good for me too, to take a leaf from Dot's book and go and 'breathe some air'.

Elina had always wanted children. From a very young age she felt she was destined for motherhood, and she dearly wanted to have a child to bring joy to our lives; but no matter how we tried, and at first we had *really* tried, nothing had happened. It couldn't have been down to me, Elina must have had something wrong with her workings.

Now we had the little flower shop, work took a great deal of our energies. I was travelling far and wide. Elina was getting concerned. She consulted doctors and she was told that fertility treatment on the NHS was possible, but that there was a long, long waiting list. There were, however, options in going to Europe; but that would have to be financed privately and could be £5,000 to £6,000 per treatment, and with no guarantees. It may as well have been on a different planet. Elina started to look into the possibilities of adoption. Well, I went along with it. I wanted an empire, not a family; in fact I felt quietly relieved that IVF was so expensive. I worried that perhaps a family would hamper our ambitions for the business, but I really, truly, did love Elina, and the thought of children kept her happy. *Why kill the dream?* I started to spend more time away from home, on business.

During that time Dot noticed a marked deterioration in her father's health, causing her to increase his care package as she was finding it more and more difficult to cope. Although these arrangements did cost substantially more money, she said that her pension, plus the state pension, and her savings were sufficient that she didn't have to worry, at least about the immediate future. It did mean, however, that Dot had more time in which she was available to help Elina, as the home care people preferred her to be out of their way. They actually said, 'Why don't you take some time for yourself, let's say mornings and all day Fridays,' which she was actually grateful for, although she did feel a little guilty about it. The extra bit of money she earned from the shop didn't hurt either.

Elina, herself, was becoming obsessed 'I just need to go upstairs for five minutes,' she would say, and then come back in an hour or so looking really depressed. Her manner changed. Her general attitude to life had been upbeat and looking forward, positive. Lately she was tired, not so much physically, more like life had beaten her and she no longer wanted to fight it. She seemed to have disappointed herself somehow. I was as supportive as I could be, certainly at first, but I was away for a lot of the time. I didn't realise, until Dot told me, that when she was alone she filled her time pouring over adoption agency photographs and stories and her mind would be on cute babies instead of on work; until a customer wanting help would jolt her out of it, or a delivery needed her attention.

Having Dot around the place proved very useful, to both of us, particularly if Elina felt she needed to go and do a little more research from time to time. Dot could keep things running smoothly and report back to me if things got too bad, and I – to be absolutely honest it was getting me down. Every time I was alone with Elina there was only one topic of conversation and I had come to dread spending time with her. Any excuse to be away from home was a blessing to me, and a relief. I could relax away from the knowledge that was killing me. I didn't really want a child. To tell her that though, would kill her, and I loved her, so I kept running away from it. I felt caught between two things, both of which gave me pain.

I carried on working hard, trying, with limited success, to build the company. I hated the, very necessary, daily appointments; they were somewhat demeaning. I was having to be obsequious and wait until people were willing to see me so that I could beg for business. This was not how I saw myself. I was a strong, fit, intelligent man with drive. My father had taken a big risk bringing us to London, far away from friends and family back home in Jamaica. Perhaps I felt the need to justify my presence. Perhaps I needed to mean something.

It has to be said that I was fairly attractive, and I most certainly had more success with managers who were both young and female, than with those who were not. It was also a good thing that I had access to bouquets of flowers for gifts; on the books they were samples, but we all know what they were, otherwise any money earned would have been quickly swallowed up. I found it easy to flatter female secretaries into finding a window in their boss's diary for an appointment. Occasionally, getting that appointment took a little more than flowers and flattery. Sometimes it was an evening in the pub, sometimes a meal out, and as I wasn't usually expected home until very late, if at all, sometimes it was a little more.

Then I met Abigail.

Abigail was stunning, and she knew it. And she made the most of it. She was twenty-eight, single, living in her brother-in-law's house, and bored. She worked part time, so that she could contribute to the household expenses, she said, and enjoy a night out from time to time. Only, those times had developed shorter gaps between them over the few years that she had had her own money.

Abigail was fun. Abigail was dangerous. I came across her while I was touting for business in one of the many offices that spread across north London. After the usual chat up and the promise of a bunch of flowers, I don't know why, instinct perhaps, but I introduced myself as David.

'David – David Lawrence, it's nice to meet you.' It was the first name that came to mind.

'Abigail Derzel, you've certainly brightened up my day.' It must have been something in her beautiful green eyes; that twinkle that says, 'I'm on if you are', and I held her hand just a fraction longer than necessary. She caught on fast, she looked me straight in the eye, the edge of a smile flirting at me. I couldn't resist, 'Perhaps we could make your day last a little longer then.'

'I don't finish 'til six, and I will need to freshen up.'

I thought she was pretty fresh as it was.

'Tell me where you... where I can pick you up.'

'I think you already have sir.' She fluttered her eyes.

I wasn't doing anything pressing, and to be honest the thought of going back home to talk about children – again, didn't fill me with joy. She wrote her address down on a piece of paper from her notepad, folded it, and passed it to me.

Without taking my eyes off her for a moment, I said, trying to sound as cool as I could. 'Eight – ish?'

'Eight – ish,' she whispered. Once outside I opened my Motorola flip phone and dialled home. 'Hi Sweetheart, how's things in the shop today?'

'Just the usual,' she said quietly 'Dot's downstairs with a customer, I'm having a cup of tea.'

'Oh, okay. Look I've got a good prospect of some business here, it's a firm of solicitors, having a works do next month. I need to get a full night's sleep, I might stay over.'

'If you like, love. I'll see you tomorrow.'

'Alright, I hope you – ' the phone went dead.

I did wish she would pick herself up, I don't know but, if she had a bit of life about her, more of the Elina that I had met with at the barrow. I know it's all about children and she thinks her clock is ticking but thirty-five isn't old and, if she would just relax about it, there is more to life.

I had booked a meal out at one of the regular hotels that I knew. The Bridge Hotel and Restaurant. Not the cheapest one, but I had stayed there occasionally. It was an older pub/hotel that had been converted to make the best use of all the upstairs space; extra bedrooms and all en suite, and although it still did have a bar, it was there mainly to serve drinks to the diners. The building was painted white outside with large black lettering across the front declaring itself to the world as it passed by, in addition to the smaller traditional pub sign, left over from its previous incarnation. As well as a table, I had booked a room, a nice one. I was going to stay over whatever happened, but it didn't hurt to be prepared.

My mind wasn't on work for the rest of the day and, as soon as I completed my final appointment – unsuccessfully but I didn't care – I drove the van to The Bridge, parked it in a car park about five minutes walk away, checked in, showered, and tidied myself up. I had spent a little too much on a small bottle of Taylor's of Bond Street, my favourite aftershave. I hoped it would be worth it.

Come seven thirty in the evening and I was ready. I decided to take a taxi. Yes, again, it would cost a bit, but I didn't want to arrive on her doorstep in a van, particularly with the shop name and phone number all over it.

I arrived at the address she had given me in plenty of time, asked the cab driver to wait for a moment and stood looking at the house. It was a large Victorian styled double fronted house with a high hedge, next to a church.

I opened the gate and went up the somewhat imposing steps to the front door and rang the bell. The door opened almost immediately and Abigail stood there, as if she'd been waiting to make an entrance, or exit in this case. She looked fabulous; she stood there in a tight pink halter topped dress with what I think they call a handkerchief hem, and a totally unnecessary belt, not that I took particular notice of the detail, as the material itself was so breath-catchingly sheer. She had a little clutch bag and shoes to match and a pashmina draped over her arms. I supposed that was just in case she got cold, but I tell you, I was getting hot. As the door closed behind her, I caught a glimpse of another woman stomping away back to the innards of the house, whom I assumed was her sister, but at that moment she was not what held my attention. We got into the taxi, and set off. I had already told the driver where we were going. I wasn't sure we'd get there safely though as he couldn't take his eyes off the rear view mirror.

The evening was wonderful, everything worked. The food

was good, the jokes funny, Abigail was as intoxicating as the wine, the music was heady, and the body language, off the scale. When we finished our meal, I didn't even have to ask, I went to the reception desk, picked up the key, and she followed me like a ticking bomb all the way to the room.

The next morning, I needed that breakfast, and it was gratifying to see her heartily devouring her food, in much the same way as we had devoured each other the previous night. I booked a taxi for her journey home and when it took her away, I walked across and down the road to where I had parked the van, and set off for the happiest day's work I'd had for a very long time.

Over the next couple of months or so, the manager of The Bridge Hotel came to know Mr David Lawrence and Abigail Derzel very well; he regularly provided us with a nice evening meal, a modest bottle of wine, and accommodation for the night. Business was picking up for Lucas's Lupins, so the van was less available for my use as Elina needed to use it for deliveries. With reasons for using taxis becoming more difficult to be convincing about, as well as becoming quite a drain on resources, I bought a ten year old Vauxhall cavalier; dark blue, one of the last one's made. It was a very good price but, with an eye out for any eventualities, I added a substantial amount to the receipt that I gave to Dot for my emergency fund. Despite raised eyebrows at spending that much on a car, I got away with it – 'It's a classic, very low mileage.' – 'Fantastic example of an iconic model, one of the last ones made,' etc etc. I'd had it about a week, when I told Elina, 'I'd better do the rounds over the next couple of days, keep in touch with the customers, you know, and I'll be able to take samples.'

'Right you are love,' Elina responded, happily. 'There's not too much on, and it'll give you a chance to try out the car.'

'Let's see if I can't land a big one this time, eh.'

'Not too big. We'd never cope. Dot and me.'

The car suited me. A lot of reps drove them. It was a good looking car. It looked impressive after a good polish, but didn't stand out too much as there were a lot of them still on the road. I spent the day going round to potential customers, booked into The Bridge to freshen up, then drove my new car to show it off to Abigail.

Life was good. Orders were flowing, if not flooding in. I had agreed with Elina to start along the adoption road. Although she knew that things wouldn't happen quickly, she hoped they would happen, and I was good at stalling. So she was happy. As she was happy, I was happy. I had to spend a lot of trips away from home, and so Abigail was very happy. The manager of The Bridge was happy. Abigail even mentioned the 'L' word. Until one day in early spring, it all changed. She turned and looked at me. She paused.

'David,' she started, 'there's something I need to tell you, I meant to last night, but we did get a bit carried away.'

'What's that?' I asked.

'I'm expecting.'

'Expecting what?'

'Expecting! – I'm pregnant.'

'What? – No, you can't be. – I mean there hasn't been time. When? Are you sure?'

'I thought you'd be pleased.'

'Yes, I am – but it couldn't, we were careful.'

'Not that first time,' said Abigail, grinning. 'There was nothing at all careful about that.'

'I know but – '

'And it only takes once.'

Then we got into the cavalier and I drove thoughtfully back to the house. She had held off from telling me sooner as she was nervous about my reaction.

Well now!

Things weren't yet becoming obvious, but Abigail was worried. I reassured her that everything would be okay. *What else could I say?* She was single, and young with no ties. So that wasn't the problem. Her problem was her brother-in-law. He was the pastor of the church next door to where they lived, and he advocated that people should live a straight and narrow life, spiritually and morally speaking, despite the fact that the church was a very vibrant place full of joy and song every Sunday. Abigail didn't think he'd realised yet, but it wouldn't be long, and then the furies would awake in him. She had to move out, certainly temporarily, possibly permanently. 'Could she come and live with me?' *Noooo!* I screamed inside, that was not going to happen.

'Abi, I can't. The lease is up on my place, I'm going to have to bunk on my friend Adey's sofa until I can find somewhere, and with work sending me away on courses now, I have nothing to offer you.'

'David! What am I going to do?'

'We could do something about it, couldn't we?'

She looked shocked, 'What do you mean, do something?'

'Well, they can get rid of it quite easily nowadays can't they?'

'I suppose they can, but David, what if I don't want to?'

'That's ridiculous, we can't have a baby. Is there no-one that you know that can help out? Relatives?'

'Not really.' There was a moment there. She looked at me differently.

'Ridiculous?' she said. 'I do have a cousin up north, somewhere called Otley in Yorkshire, but I haven't seen them for years.'

I was clutching at straws, 'Well for now, the best, the only solution, I suppose, is to get in touch. Give them some story. You're ill. You need a rest, away from the city. Only for a little while, until – ' I indicated her stomach, I just couldn't say the words, 'Then come back and by that time, I'll have something sorted.'

'What would I say to Ben?'

I began to smell onions, and that odd 'not here', sensation began to affect me. This hadn't happened for a long time. I sat down.

'David! David! Are you listening? David!'

'Who?'

'You. David. What am I going to say?'

What was she talking about?

'My brother in law – the pastor. What should I do?'

I don't know how long it was until I remember saying, 'But I'm not – Pasta? – David?'

I came back. 'I'm sorry, I sometimes. I kind of blackout – without falling over. I don't know what it is. I'm okay now, it's over.'

'How often does this happen,' she asked.

'Not very, only when there's stress over something. Don't say anything to anybody though. If they find out I won't be able to drive, and I can't have that.'

Abigail looked at me strangely, 'You know what. I might be able to do something about that for you. When we've sorted everything out.'

'Oh, well, I don't know, maybe – yes. Could you?' I wasn't really listening, I needed the current problem dealing with. 'You could tell your brother-in-law that someone there is ill, and they need your help. Something like that.'

'I'm not sure.'

'What else is there?'

'And you'll sort things out here, for us, when I come back? Do you promise?'

'Of course.' I would indeed sort something. 'I have heard that Yorkshire is cheaper than here anyway, I can let you have a little money, for costs, you know.' There went the emergency fund.

I didn't see Abigail for quite a while. She went north to her cousin's, to 'sort' things, and I settled back into my routine. Business was looking up and I got a contract with a church, not far from the shop, to supply flowers. Only we had to do the flower arranging as well, so once it was set up, I left that one to Elina.

The adoption saga was ongoing and Elina had got me decorating the second bedroom as a playroom. It was daft, of course, as we had no idea whether we could adopt. If we could, we didn't know whether it would be a boy or girl, or even what age. Elina was just hoping for a baby. I was dragging my heels. I wasn't committed to the idea at all. We had registered with some adoption agencies in person and been told 'We will be in touch.'

Abigail and I had bought each other matching mobile phones before she left, they were the Samsung slider type, where the top slides up to reveal the keypad underneath, very small and discreet, and it meant that we could keep in touch securely, which reassured her and minimised my risk. To be really honest, I kept jollying her along with news about my search for a flat, courses I was going on, and the rest of this fictitious life I was getting embroiled in. I didn't think it was that important really as, when she came back, I'd give her a story about how hard it was, difficulty with my documents, something like that; then I thought we could pick up where we left off.

She was telling me all about life in Otley, about how shop-keepers actually talk to you, unlike the ones she was used to in town. She didn't seem to say much about hospitals or clinics or how she was getting along with that. I didn't know how long one could leave it safely, or legally, but surely not as long as this? Or maybe she wanted to wipe the whole thing from her mind and just have a holiday. She was away far longer than I'd thought she would be, but that was alright, I could wait.

One Monday, late morning, just after I'd left a meeting with a funeral director, the slider rang. It took me a moment to dig it out from its permanent home, buried deep in the glove box in the car. 'Hi Abi, how's things oop North?' My usual greeting, sorry.

'Hello David, I hope everything's ready because we're coming home. We'll be catching the train on Friday morning.' I was stunned for a moment. This was sudden, I mean I know it had been a long time, just over seven months to be more precise, but Friday!

'Wait a minute – we? Who's coming with you?'

'Our daughter.' She waited.

'Daughter? But we haven't – you didn't do it did you? Oh shit. Sorry – no, it's a surprise. But – but what are we going to do with a daughter?'

'Don't worry, it'll be alright. I'll explain everything when I get there. You have got us somewhere nice together, haven't you?'

'I thought it would be just you though, and we could go back to – It's been really difficult, I have tried real hard. I don't suppose we could? You know, the way it was, at your sister's house. I haven't really been – '

'Oh David. Well you'll have to get your skates on then, we're coming on Friday. You've got almost a week, to find somewhere. I can't wait to see you and for you two to meet for the first time. David, she is beautiful.'

Oh, Hell! What was I going to do? I rushed around the nearest estate agencies, flat rental agencies, even bedsits would do. Work had to be put aside. It took me three full days, but I found a couple of places that would do, and I could move straight in, with minimum fuss. I had to find a deposit of course, but if I told Elina that the car had let me down and the garage fees were astronomical, she wouldn't know any different. The paperwork was no problem, I had made contacts in several offices who were more than willing to do me a favour and mock up some receipts. Fine. That was now, but it wouldn't work long term, I had a wife, and a business! This would destroy them both. They say desperate situations need desperate remedies, and an idea started to grow in my mind. It would tidy everything up, nearly everyone would be happy. I went to find Adey.

Friday. Abigail and the baby were on their way, in fact they shouldn't be long now. I'd found a place in Balfour Grove. It had two bedrooms but it was in a real state. I'd found Adey, given him some money and got his help in cleaning up the place and getting some secondhand furniture. The stuff in the place was filthy and mostly broken, although it was 'furnished' according to the rental office.

I had been going home as much as I could, because I knew I'd have to have at least a couple of days with Abigail. Well I mean, after seven months. While I was there I made out a cheque from the business account, which unfortunately had to be in Elina's name, so I copied her signature and left the payee blank. I gave it to Adey, he could fill in whatever name he wanted on it.

Abigail arrived at Kings Cross. Amazingly, the train was on time, and I picked them up in the car. The traffic was hell at that time of day, as everyone was leaving work for the weekend, and it took as long to get to the flat as the train journey had. Well nearly. I know she was disappointed with the place. It was rough, but what could she expect with a few days notice? I met the baby, Rebecca she'd called it. After some long lost relative. I made lots of fuss and took loads of pictures.

I'd told Elina I had to go to Milton Keynes on Friday to the head office of a company of event organisers. I said it wouldn't be worth coming back late on the Saturday, but that I'd get the first available train back on Sunday. Dot didn't work on

Sundays so she'd be on her own, but she'd smiled and said I could do with some time to unwind after a hard week.

Saturday was a lovely day, cool, but with promise; the sun was already peeping out from behind the clouds. A perfect day for a walk in the park.

'Abi, darling, why don't we take Rebecca out for some fresh air, it'll get us out of this place for a bit?'

'That's a good idea David, let me wrap her up warm.' Warm? It wasn't cold! 'We can go and feed the ducks,' I added.

So we went to the park, it wasn't far, just a short walk from the flat. It was already warming up, there were a lot of people about. We had a lovely time. Come one o'clock we were getting hungry, and Rebecca needed feeding too, so we found a shady spot, settled there, and I went off to a kiosk we'd spotted to get some sandwiches.

As I returned I saw Abi, feeding Rebecca with the bottle she had prepared. To be honest, they did look cute. We had one of those disposable cameras, like in *Mission Impossible*. I took a picture, for old time's sake, whatever. 'Look, I'll take over, if you like. Why don't you get us some coffee?' I said.

'Alright, do you know how to do it, be careful, don't choke her, a little at a time.' Abigail picked up the camera, took a couple of steps, stopped and took a snap of me with Rebecca, then she tossed the little camera back to me 'Alright, I know, don't be long though.'

She went. I took the remains of my sandwich to the pond and tore it up into little pieces; we don't want to choke the ducks either, now do we? There were others doing the same thing, those ducks never had it so good. I made some joke to a lady near me about being surprised the ducks could still float after all that bread, then I turned to go back. There was the rug we'd put down, just by the hedge, Rebecca's pushchair was right beside it, the little pink blanket was there on the rug, but no Rebecca. I bolted back to it, searched around, had she somehow crawled under the bush? I called, "Becca?', she wouldn't answer, she was a baby.

Then I screamed 'Rebecca!' She wasn't there. People turned, I ran. Here. There. 'Rebecca!' She was nowhere to be seen.

Others were running about too, 'What's happened?'

'My little girl. She's gone!'

Then Abi appeared and saw, rather than heard, the commotion. It only took her a second to understand. Coffee went flying; she ran screaming, panicking.

'Rebecca, My baby. What happened? Where is she?'

I was sweating now. The sun wasn't so nice.

'I just – just fed the ducks. I turned round and she'd gone.'

'Where?' She screamed in my face.

'I don't know, just gone!'

The police came, took statements, told us, me, 'Don't blame yourselves. These things happen from time to time, and families are usually reunited quite quickly.'

Abi was ashen, a WPC was calming her down, people were being helpful, looking about at anyone carrying a baby. Nothing. The police told us to go home, they would take it very seriously and put the word out to all officers in the area. It shouldn't be long.

For almost two days, we sat in that flat, she blaming me even if she didn't say so. Me feeling guilty, neither of us knew what to do. I left on Sunday evening, I couldn't stay any longer. 'I have to get back, I need to work.' I told her.

'Not now, please God, not now. David, I need you here.'

But I went.

~

After the park incident I went back home, to Elina. I'll be honest, I couldn't cope. I was worried sick. However, I slept better than I had in a long time, I suppose it must have been the familiar sounds in and around the shop. Then on Monday morning I woke as usual, to the sound of Elina coming back in from the market.

I got up and started breakfast. She came up the stairs as I put the mug of tea on the table, 'It was busy down there this morning, thanks for this Dev,' she said, hugging the mug.

'It's nice to be home,' I replied.

'Well, don't get too used to sitting around here.' Elina laughed, 'There's plenty of work to be done, and I can't do it on my own. How did it all go in Milton Keynes?'

Milton Keynes? What was she talking about? Oh shit, of course. With everything going on, I'd forgotten that's where I was supposed to have been.

'Pretty boring really,' I recovered, 'They are a firm of events organisers. Working for different concerns all over the country.'

Elina was interested, 'What sort of events?' she asked.

'Well, all kinds they said. It might be a fashion show in Edinburgh one week and a catering exhibition in Swansea the next. But I felt that what they were willing to pay and what they were wanting was a bit beyond us at the moment.'

'So, no contracts at all then?'

'It wasn't a "No", it was more of a "later" sort of thing. We're not really geared up for business on that scale yet, and, as I said, they weren't exactly going to throw money at us.'

We finished our cups of tea; then the shop bell rang downstairs putting an end to the conversation. To my relief to be honest. I don't like lying. Sometimes you have to lie, to be fair, but I don't like it and the sooner it stops the better.

Life settled back into the old routine quickly enough. I spent some time helping in the shop and some time out on the road. Things were actually looking up, business wise, and we were picking up one or two contacts here and there. Funeral directors, party supplies, the odd hotel do.

At first I phoned Abigail, as often as my situation would allow. No news. She was distraught still, I felt so bad putting the phone down on her. *What was going on?*

The search went on for months. It was on the local TV news for a bit, but then there was a spate of murders between rival gangs which took precedence. There were a few sightings, follow ups, but ultimately nothing. Then I saw Adey's face on the TV. I didn't see it for long and didn't know whether it was because he was a victim, a suspect or a contestant on X Factor, but it made me think.

Abigail moved back in with her sister and brother-in-law, and our meet ups became less frequent. There was something between us. Something, now, that would always be there. It was in the way she looked at me. I was to blame for it all. She found it hard to move on.

~

Then one day during this time – a Friday in fact, a busy morning – Elina and I had just stopped for a breather and a mug of tea, when the phone rang. I sat still. She looked at me for a moment, willing me to answer it. Then she sighed, put the mug down and reached for the receiver.

'Who?' then, a moment, 'Yes, yes it is me, I mean yes Elina Lucas. I am.' She turned, 'It's the agency.'

'What agency?' I replied.

She glared. 'The adoption agency, idiot!'

I tensed, 'But which one?' She ignored me.

Then she lit up like a touch-paper. 'Yes, yes of course. Oh, that's wonderful. This is so quick though. Oh, I see, well, yes. Wednesday? We will be here, yes we'll close on Wednesday, all day ha-ha! Thank you. Thank you. Bye – bye.' The fuse had been lit, now the explosion.

'Devon! It's a baby, they've found a baby for us. A baby girl, they're bringing her on Wednesday. Apparently the mother was having mental health issues and they had our details and forms and that, and we matched. Oh, Devon. I love you so much. A Baby!'

The agency had said the baby's name was Maeve. Elina loved that baby and wouldn't change a thing about her, so Maeve it stayed. Maeve had arrived, not at the agency offices, but on a wet Wednesday afternoon in October at the door of the flower shop. Her arrival was welcomed by the cheerful jangling of the shop bell above the door. The woman in the car just handed her over with some official looking documents and a warning that there was a probationary period and they would be in touch regularly, then I took her up the stairs and into the flat above the shop. Elina was a different person. She changed in an instant. She was born to motherhood. I took a moment and filed the papers in the back of the cupboard.

After the magic phone call, Elina and I had moved as if in a frenzy, painting and decorating her room, buying everything and anything that any baby could possibly want. Ever. Whether or not we could afford it. Nothing was too good for Maeve Lucas.

After the initial excitement of Maeve's arrival, life settled back into a similar routine as before, not the same, similar. Well, we tried. I thought that life would go on the same, or near enough, just with one extra mouth to feed; which I was prepared to accept. What I wasn't prepared to accept, were the sleepless nights because the baby was crying, the changing of nappies, the curtailment of my travel plans because we needed an extra hand whenever there was an appointment at the doctor's, and there were many appointments.

I had to help out in the shop too, with the baby alarm by my side, because Elina was tired. Hell, I was tired too. These days she did seem to be tired a lot of the time, especially when I needed a little 'attention'.

Then the letter arrived. It came through the shop letterbox, but not via the postman. It was hand delivered and it just said 'Devon' on the front. Fortunately it didn't arrive first thing, and Elina was out. I came downstairs for something, I don't remember exactly what it was – perhaps it was the letterbox itself – and it was lying on the floor. I opened it up. I didn't recognise the writing. It was more of a childish scrawl really. There was only one page.

I want the money like you promised. Now.

That was it, but folded inside was a baby picture. I knew what it meant though, he hadn't been on X Factor or a victim. I didn't have any money. At least not enough to deal with this, without it becoming clear and obvious to all concerned. I decided to ignore it, for a while, to give myself time to think.

In the meantime I had enough to think about. All the work I'd done, was likely to be brought to nothing. The contacts lost, dreams of an empire dissolved before my eyes. I couldn't find time to think. Whenever I was doing one job, I was needed somewhere else. When I was making up bouquets, Elina wanted the feed making up or she would need something from the shop, supplies for the baby, medicines from the chemist's. Then it was 'Collect her from the nursery,' and 'This place is a mess, you never tidy!'

Tidy? What with the lack of sleep, and the constant demands, when's there ever time? And why can't *you* lift your arse off the settee once in a while to push the vacuum around? Oh, *you're* tired.

I had been in touch regularly with Abigail, who had moved back in with her sister after only a very short time on her own in 'our' place. Over time things had improved between us and it became a relief to get away, on those occasional days when I could, to go and take her out, and find some 'relief'; even though the bridge between us was imperfect and that the darkness was still in her.

Eventually, and in reality it didn't take very long, I didn't seem to matter to Elina any more. I was convenient. She'd got what she wanted. It was Maeve first, always, then the shop, then me. After constantly feeling I was being told to be anywhere other than where I was, or to do anything other than what I was actually engaged on, I decided I would finally be somewhere else.

I packed a few things, left a short note – at least that way she wouldn't be waiting for me – and I went out on a visit to sort out an order that had a problem.

I wasn't going back.

I called Abigail, we still used the sliders to ring from, even though they were becoming a bit out of date now. They were cheap, they still worked, and we arranged to go out somewhere. I booked The Bridge Hotel, for old times' sake I suppose, and they had entertainment. Tonight was Il Divo, one of Abigail's favourites. They had been happy to take a last minute reservation without asking for a deposit. I knew there was always the possibility that I may have to cancel it, but as usual preparation is key. Then I sorted out the bit of flower shop business that needed reorganising. Even though I had decided not to go back to the shop, there was no reason to leave people up the creek, was there? Back to the hotel and I got myself ready, shower, shave, and of course my favourite Taylor's sandalwood after shave. I was still driving the cavalier, though it was beginning to look a bit worn down, even a good polish couldn't shine the rusty bits.

I drove it to the vicarage, I suppose it was still called that, even though technically Abi's brother-in-law wasn't actually a vicar, he was a pastor, but I'd never heard of a pastorage. I parked in front and went to the door. Deep breath.

Her sister Hannah opened the door 'Oh, hello. – Abi!' she called. 'Come in for a minute. – David, isn't it? Have we met? I seem to recognise you from somewhere?'

'No – no I've never seen you before. I'm not from round here,' I said as I quickly looked away, towards the car.

'Oh. Sorry.' She was very polite. 'Excuse me, I'm just in the middle of settling Elliot into bed, Abi, David's here!' Hannah stepped aside to allow me entry and led Elliot, already in his pyjamas toward the stairs.

There was another child crying from upstairs. 'Coming, darling,' called Hannah. 'Mummy's coming.' She turned to Abi, on her way from the back kitchen, 'Could you at least be careful, when you're back, you know what he can be like. We'll talk then?' Hannah said.

'Whenever you're ready, of course,' petulantly from Abigail.

'Abi, don't, the kids, I've got to – '

'Whatever,' said Abigail. 'I'm all yours David, lead the way.' She swept past the conversation, and waited, regally, at the door.

As I turned, I noticed a familiar looking envelope on the shelf near the door. It hadn't been opened and I could see the name on the front 'David L.' in a childish scrawl. Abigail saw me notice it. 'Oh, that came, about a week ago. It must be for you, I don't know anyone else called David, but why would it come here?'

There were very few people who knew me as David L, and fewer still who knew they could reach me here. She picked it up and handed it to me. I stuffed it in my pocket, 'What's it all about David?'

I had felt the envelope as I pocketed it. There was a smaller stiff card inside.

'Aren't you going to open it?'

I pulled it out again and ripped the end, half drew out the contents. It was a photograph folded inside a single sheet.

'No it's nothing, not even for me. It's asking for donations.' I shoved it deep into my pocket again. 'Tonight my lady, we travel in style. Ta-da!' Lighthearted was probably best. 'Your carriage awaits.' I opened the passenger door for her and, with a raised eyebrow, she almost glided over the rust spot on the sill and into the seat.

The evening, with a coolish atmosphere, and a very large and somewhat over ornate dining room cowing things a little, didn't start out very promising; but it turned out to be excellent, with a very enjoyable meal, accompanied by a better bottle of wine than usual. So much better that we had another, and a very special performance featuring *Il Divo* classical singing quartet helped to warm things up; and afterwards we happily supported each other up to the double room on the first floor where, once inside, our clothes lay where they fell and we enjoyed a long passionate embrace.

While Abigail showered, I retrieved my jacket and took the envelope out of my pocket.

Five days. if you play with matches, you will get burned.

∾

I slept the sleep of the innocent and awoke to a sharp pain in my buttock, and a woolly feeling head; she slapped me hard. 'What the fucking hell was that?'

Abigail put something in her bag and said, 'Those little episodes that you have. Well you won't be having any more. You can thank me later.'

'What did you do?' *What the hell was going on?*

'Just a little thing, but it will sort you out. Now come along.'

I was feeling a little the worse for wear, not to say sore. Nothing a shower and a good breakfast couldn't cure though. Abi was already up and dressed.

'You're up with the larks aren't you, you must have the constitution of an ox.' She smiled a closed sort of smile but didn't speak, 'Perhaps you've been too quick, you've got quite a smudge on the side of your face. Is it a smudge?'

She wiped at it with a towel, it didn't come off. 'No. It's a bruise. I didn't do it last night did I? I am so sorry.'

She went into the en-suite for a long moment, and came out again, pristine, complete with make up. Bruise gone. As we walked out past reception, the clerk smiled.

'Good morning again, Miss, I hope everything turned out alright for you?' he said.

'Yes,' said Abigail, without looking at him, 'We had a lovely stay.' We went into the hotel car park, found the car and headed off.

'I hope we catch Hannah and the kids before they set off for the day.'

'Where would they go?' I asked.

'Hannah has to work you know, and the kids need to go to nursery or school. Whichever, I need to talk to her.' The rest of the journey was in silence.

The road to the house was blocked with vehicles. Two fire engines, and two police cars were in the way. It wasn't until we got past the first fire engine that we saw the house. Abigail's first reaction was shock, and then disbelief. The house was a burnt out ruin. Wisps of smoke were still rising from various places.

'Where are they?' she asked of a fireman resting by the first of the engines. 'The people from inside. Where are they?'

He was exhausted and filthy, 'I don't know love.' He looked up, 'Who are you anyway?'

She was extremely calm, 'I live here,' then she couldn't hold it in 'This is my house, where are my family? – I need to find something.'

He almost came to attention 'Er – no miss, you can't go in there, it's too dangerous.'

'No there's a suitcase, with baby things.'

'Baby things,' the policeman almost shouted, 'There's a baby? John!' he suddenly shouted. 'John! Did anyone find a baby?'

'What?' the fireman shouted back as he turned to the ruined building. Then Abigail realised what she'd done.

'No, no, no. Baby clothes. No baby. – There is no baby.' The words hurt her more than she expected. 'There is no baby.'

The policeman shouted to the fireman 'False alarm. Everyone's accounted for.'

'You don't want to go scaring us like that miss. Any belongings can be collected later, if anything has survived. I'll probably be here, or my colleague, when the fire-boys have made it safe.'

Abigail asked, 'Where have my family gone?'

'The ambulance took them. I'd try the hospital miss.' said the PC.

'All of them?' She was starting to panic. 'Were they all right, was anybody hurt? I mean badly. I...' She ran out of questions. She wanted answers.

'I don't know,' the firemen replied, 'if you want any more information, you probably need to speak to the crew manager.' He pointed over to the driveway and indicated a fireman talking to another police officer. 'Over there.' Abigail, didn't even think to thank him, but ran to where he had indicated.

'This is – was my house, I mean I live here. What happened?

Where are they? My sister and her kids, and her husband, the pastor?'

'Alright John,' the police officer said, 'You carry on with what you can.' The fireman nodded, cast a glance at Abigail and walked off toward the second engine.

'I'm sorry, Ma'am, who are you?'

'Abigail, Derzel, This was my sister's house. Where are they? Are they alright?'

'The ambulance took them off to the Queen Elizabeth hospital. It was a very serious fire ma'am. I would advise going there for any updates, all the information I have is that the fire started during the night when they were all asleep.'

Almost before he had finished speaking Abigail was running back, 'David, to the hospital – Queen Elizabeth hospital – as quick as you can. The ambulance took them all there. He said it was really bad. Hurry. We were sleeping all night while this was happening, I can't believe it.'

I started the engine, threw the car into gear and hit the accelerator hard. I ripped up through the gears, and tore through the streets as fast as I could. It took ten minutes to get there. While I circled the car park, searching for a space, Abigail leapt out and into A&E. The waiting area was full, she went straight over to the queue at the reception window. I left the car at the roadside and ran in, just in time to hear her shouting at the window 'My sister and family have just come in an ambulance. I've got to see them. Where are they?'

'What name was it please ma'am?'

'Derzel. No, Saphan, My name's Derzel. Saphan. Ben and Hannah Saphan and the children. They came after the fire.'

'They would have gone straight to the burns unit, if it was a fire. Go through the double doors and follow the green signs.'

She rushed through, hardly seeing the people busying themselves in her way. I followed a little slower, only in order to avoid knocking people flying though. Fortunately they all got out of Abigail's way. Her eyes were focused on the signs overhead. Green, green, green? She called out, to no-one in particular, but everyone in general, 'Burns unit, where's the burns unit?' A kind soul in a blue uniform caught her arm, and pointed her down a corridor,

'Down that way, and right at the end.'

Without looking at who it was, she hurried in the direction she was shown until she saw the green sign pointing to the right. She pushed the door, it didn't budge. Then she noticed the buzzer at the side and pressed it impatiently. I caught up with her while she was tapping her foot and looking from side to side, then a disinterested, disembodied voice answered.

'Hello.'

'I – My sister has been brought here in an ambulance.' Before she had even finished speaking, the door buzzed again and this time as she pushed, it swung open. The desk was in an open area at the end of a short corridor, with doors on either side all the way along. As she approached it she said, 'Saphan, my sister and her husband, were brought in an ambulance with the children, a little boy and girl?'

'Excuse me, just a moment,' the nurse at the desk said.

Just then 'Abigail – Abigail. Here, it's me Ben. In here,' came Ben's voice, from behind her. She turned as Ben looked out of a small lounge. He looked rough. She went in. I waited in the corridor, but the door was open and I could hear every word.

'They've gone – there's just Elliot. He's in there.' I suppose he pointed.

'Gone where? Ben, where is Hannah?'

'She's gone, and little Rachel. I could only get Elliot out. I tried – I tried.' His voice crumpled.

'No! They can't be. I saw them just yesterday.'

'They wouldn't let me go in. I couldn't save them.' Ben was crying.

'But how? What happened?'

'I don't know, they were asleep upstairs, I must have dozed off. I woke up coughing and the whole place was full of smoke. Elliot was at the top of the stairs, burning. Abigail, he was on fire. His hands were burning. I got him out and tried to go back, but they stopped me.'

I moved so I could see through the partially open door. Abigail opened her arms to him, and hugged him as tight as she could, as if she could hold her whole family if only it was tight enough. But she couldn't. A young doctor went in.

'Mr Saphan?'

'Yes,' said Ben 'This is my sister-in-law, Abigail.'

'Abigail...?'

'Derzel, Abigail Derzel.'

'Well, Ms Derzel, Mr Saphan, would you come with me please? The consultant would like a word with you. His office is this way.'

They came out and went with him, I stepped away as soon as I saw them start to move. They didn't even glance my way. I wandered about while I waited. I find hospitals to be alien places. Everybody seems busy, but you can never find anyone to help, they all have different coloured uniforms, some don't have uniforms at all. If you're a nurse, people seem to call you staff and doctors are called mister if they've got an office, and there are so many signs, like a maze with arrows all going in different directions.

I don't know how long it had been before Abigail found me. 'David, thank goodness. Ben's here, the pastor, but Hannah and the baby didn't...' Tears welled up and her throat constricted 'Elliot's here in the hospital, with terrible burns, and I have nowhere to go. Could I stay at yours for a few days, while I sort myself out?'

That stopped me. She continued, 'Ben has been found a temporary place by the church elders for when the hospital releases him, but I need somewhere urgently.'

'No! I'm sorry, but it's not possible.'

'Not possible? David? It's only a couple of days. I don't want to move in.'

'No, it's not that. It's my sister, she's staying with me.'

'Your sister? I didn't know you had a sister. Surely she wouldn't mind?'

'There's not room, her daughter is staying too, and it's a very small flat.'

I started to walk away. Hesitantly she followed.

'I only need a couch. Just a couple of days.'

'It's just not possible. Sorry, I can't help.'

'Can't or won't?'

'No, honestly. It just can't happen. You'll have to go with the pastor, wherever he's going to stay. Won't the church do something?'

'I suppose they will have to. What's going on David?'

I walked faster. 'I have to get the car, it's parked on yellows, there weren't any spaces. Look, I'll call you when you're settled. I left something at the hotel,' and with that I turned and left Abigail standing there, looking stunned.

~

Things hadn't gone well. When I had left the hospital that day, I had nowhere to go. I couldn't go back to Elina, that road was closed. Abigail. No, I'd just walked out of her life. Where then? The only other person I knew well enough was Adey, and he was looking for me. And I didn't want to be found. I had the car. That would have to do, temporarily at best. So, I drove out to a quiet spot outside of town (beyond that magical barrier that is the M25) – the sign said Woking – and parked up. I needed to think. I only had a little money and I didn't want to waste it all. I needed to eat, I needed a job, fuel, and somewhere to live. I slept that night in the car. There were some public toilets not far away. I used those to freshen up in the morning. I couldn't do that again. The only positive thing was that I felt great, alive, no aches and pains from the cramped car; I thought I'd feel dreadful. I had to do something.

My best plan of action was to use my strengths. I headed for a pub, a busy pub. While I was still clean, and had enough for a drink or two. I waited until just after opening time, I thought I could pick up some woman and get in with her for a while. I was desperate, but I was good, and, oddly, I felt powerful. I stood just inside the doorway of The Bright Star public house and watched. I was looking for an older woman on her own, of tidy appearance. A couple of minutes in and Bingo! I will spare you the details, tawdry as they were. I went home with her, and spent the next few weeks with her whilst thinking about what to do. I eventually moved on when she started complaining about my contribution toward the bills, and found myself further south, in Andover. I wasn't impressed with Andover, but then I don't suppose Andover was very impressed by me. I parked up, and looked for a decent pub once more.

So it went on. I stayed with someone for a while, until I

outstayed my welcome, and then moved on further away each time. Different pubs, different towns. I found odd jobs here and there for cash; but I'm afraid most of it was spent on drink, looking for my next 'patron'. That's what I told myself anyway. In reality, the drink itself became the reason for going to the pub, and I was becoming less and less successful in finding a bed for the night. I kept moving onward. I became used to sleeping in the car.

Then I saw it, I had dreamed of it once as a child and there it was. A sign declaring, Devon. I must have looked a bit of a mess, because people seemed to avoid me whenever possible. I mean just walking along the street, someone would noticeably cross over. Work opportunities were drying up too, though I could still pay for necessities. Until the car broke down. It was the starter motor. I couldn't afford to have it fixed, so when I parked I made sure I was at the top of a slope, in order to bump start it to get it going again. I found a quiet lane I could park on with no questions.

I went there after the pub, I remember driving there, and then nothing much after that until I came to. The front of the car was smashed and there was a burning smell, I'd run into a tree. That was that. That car was going nowhere. That quiet lane started to get quite busy after dark. People were appearing with torches and looking in the car, then moving off to find another one. Some cars had quite a crowd around them, mostly men. I sat there for a while, and rooting around the glove box, I found the remains of a bottle of Taylors of Bond Street after shave. There wasn't much in it, but what the hell, I drank it in one. At least my breath would smell nice. It turned out that it was a popular spot for couples and would-be couples to pass some time. I removed the number plates, left the car there and hung around outside a couple of pubs. I slept on 'friend's' couches on a night by night basis, whenever I could, but without money, friends were harder to find.

That sort of set the pattern for the next few years. Living where I could, begging, doing a bit of work now and again. Not all the work was legal, I might add. In fact, to be totally honest, none of it was, but it was cash. I might add, that by this time I had changed my name a few times. I actually changed it every time I moved on. It wouldn't do to be traceable. It's a strange thing, how a life can disappear in such a way, and, it is true. Devon had disappeared. I had become this non person, through – what? Pride? Deceit? Cowardice? Alcohol? All of the above. I'd had a future. Now I only had a past. What was the point in prolonging it? Dragging it out? I was feeling very low one day as I considered my options. They weren't good. That's when I met Arthur. He just sat down beside me and started to talk. He made a commitment to me. I know, I didn't get it either. He promised he would be there every day, and he would help me back on my feet. People say things like that all the time, but Arthur stuck. He did exactly as he said he would do. Not to drag this all out too long, Arthur was with a charity called St Mungo's. They helped me with some local accommodation, a little work, and self esteem, and brought me back to life.

Part of that, the hardest part, was reconnecting with people from my past and atoning somehow. I had to think about that. They helped me to get back to London. Arthur arranged for somewhere to stay, and a job. It involved joining the team walking the streets and talking to homeless people on the way – rather like Arthur himself had done with me – and helping around the office, filing, cleaning, that sort of thing. It was a charity so they couldn't pay much, only what donations brought in, but with accommodation, and help with meals, available and all at a minimal cost, I managed.

Therefore, in line with my own commitment, late, one grey afternoon I found myself, once again, in South London, standing looking at my creation 'Lucas's Lupins'. Not directly outside, down the road a bit. I didn't want to be seen, not yet, I wasn't ready. I stayed there for a while, trying to work up the courage. Maybe I was hoping to see Elina, or Maeve. I don't know. Perhaps I needed a bit more time. I moved away a little.

I heard the police car before I saw it. The siren echoing around the buildings. I shrank back against the wall, out of habit I suppose, then looked back to where it was coming from. The blue light continued but the noise stopped right where I had just been, outside the shop. I froze. I had no idea what to do, so I did nothing. I stood there, with one or two others who had also stopped to see. Nothing happened.

Ten minutes went by, people lost interest and walked off. Except one shadowy figure that I couldn't quite see. I remained watching. Then the two officers came out with Maeve, I assumed it was her, it had been so long, and Elina. They got into the car and drove away, more sedately this time.

What the fuck!

I turned to walk away, and bumped into someone. I looked up.

'Watch where you're goin' mate.'

I looked at the face in front of me. 'Adey?'

'Sorry mate. Time's up!' he said.

THE BOOK OF BEN

I believe I was called to this ministry to heal. It was a calling directly by God, and I work very hard at it. Perhaps it's because I have always been susceptible to illness myself, particularly throughout my childhood; I do remember being bed ridden with mumps, chickenpox, and even scarlet fever at one time or another. It affected me deeply and I was conscious at the time of children all over the world suffering much worse than I. Perhaps because of that, I wanted to help them and that is why I believe that He has called me and that His Holy Spirit is with me, particularly at the healing services.

I love the church, I feel at home there, relaxed and safe in my destiny. It's not a compensation for anything, as some may have speculated. It is my world and following the will of God in this way has made me the happiest I have ever been. The church has always been full of passion and love, and everyone leaves afterwards – if not having been miraculously cured of whatever was ailing them – at least feeling spiritually fulfilled, and ready to struggle through their pain to salvation. If it be God's will.

It was at one of these healing services, or just afterwards, more than twenty years ago now, that I met Hannah. I hadn't noticed her particularly during the service and, as usual, afterwards I went to the doors to see everyone safely away. On coming back inside the church there she was.

'Er, excuse me, can I help you at all?' I asked.

She looked at me for a long moment. 'Do you believe in God's presence among us?'

What did she mean by that, I'm a pastor? 'I beg your pardon.' I was a little taken aback.

'Your sermon was full of passion and fire, very inspiring, but do you believe that God walks among us?'

It was my turn to take a moment. 'I have known God for a number of years, and He called me to His service through His only Son Christ Jesus. Yes, I believe He walks among us, He promises us that.'

'Yes, He promised that. I just wanted to be sure.'

This time, I looked at her. She was an auburn-haired woman, somewhat pale, of slender build, and a quiet determination in her piercing eyes. Now that I recall, she had sat quietly all through the proceedings even when all around her were standing and belting out songs to the glory of God. She remained in her seat afterwards, while the helpers tidied up the church – picking up hymn books etc. – and may have been there still if I hadn't approached her.

Before locking up, as she seemed disinclined to leave, I invited her into the church office attached to my house next door. We had a cup of tea and fell into a long conversation; which felt more like an interrogation to be honest.

'Where did you go to theological college?' – 'How many people come to the church regularly?' – 'Do you have an outreach programme?' – 'Is God's purpose revealed to you?' – 'How often do you have these healing services?' – 'Does God ever heal anyone?'

I felt as if I was being interviewed for something. I began to get hungry 'Look, I can offer you something to eat, if you'd like to continue this, but it would have to be in the house, there are no facilities here. Beyond the kettle that is.'

'Oh, no I certainly couldn't do that just yet. No, I should leave.'

I understood her concern, 'If you are at all worried, my secretary usually comes back with me to share an evening meal, if you feel a chaperone is necessary.' Again, that look. 'No. There is no need. There will be another time.' she said. She then stood up and left.

I must admit, she had unbalanced me, and all that evening and the next day, I just couldn't get her out of my mind. The next Sunday I spotted her early. Again she simply sat. Afterwards I approached her and chatted for a minute before she said 'I am ready now. Where would you like to take me? I must warn you I do not eat flesh.'

'Take you?' I asked, 'Yes,' she carried on, 'You asked to take me out to eat last week. I am ready now.'

'Oh, right, yes of course. Would you excuse me for a couple of seconds while I change, out of my work clothes?' That was always my little joke.

'Do they only represent you as a person at work?'

I paused. I was going to have to be careful in what I said. 'No, they represent my calling, and I have been wearing them all morning and I need to change, or I will be noticeable not only by my clothing but by my smell.' She suddenly burst into laughter. An open, honest laughter which lit up her face. She held her hand up to her face to try to cover it.

'I wanted to be sure. Certainly, take as long as you need. I shall be waiting outside.'

We had lunch, the first of many together. She seemed a different person now. She was relaxed, funny, and, dare a man of God say it, very sexy.

We fell in love. We talked of marriage and children. 'I don't hold out much hope of children, I was ill as a child and as a result, it is unlikely,' I told her.

'We must have a child,' she said, 'At the very least one child.'

Perhaps this would be the sticking point in our growing relationship. 'Must? Well, there is always hope, I suppose, but the doctors said at the time, that it was very unlikely. It's because of a very low sperm count you see.'

'Don't worry about what the doctors said. Times move on and God can heal, didn't you know, through prayer?' She smiled.

So, despite those early misgivings, we were married. Perhaps my faith wasn't as great as hers, so I tried to set up a busy, fulfilling life for us. She became pregnant almost immediately; I don't know how – I mean, I do know how – but I didn't think it possible. I'd been told my low sperm count precluded children. Nevertheless Elliot was born, the name was gender neutral, because we didn't know whether he would be a boy or a girl, and its meaning 'The Lord is my God' in Hebrew, seemed appropriate. He had to be baptised of course, so it was done at our church. Baptisms were a large part in the life of our church. I wanted to be sure that anyone finding God in this ministry should be baptised, and not just with a teaspoonful of holy water on the forehead. They should undergo the same rite of passage as Our Lord did. That meant the full immersion version involving an inflatable pool being installed in front of the pews. I would climb in and, standing waist deep in the cold water, would accept, and submerge each person in turn as they symbolically died and were reborn. For adults and children. So it was with Elliot.

Hannah started helping in the church office, doing the myriad of little jobs that need attention but, for which there never seems to be time. This was formalised by the church elders and gave her a small wage and a certain independence. She assisted where and when she could, including with the services. She became part of the community. Which is the way it should have been and, in all honesty, the way I wanted it too. Except her influence grew and it became the case that everyone I spoke to only wanted to talk to her. They asked where she was. I'd have an appointment. 'Come in Mrs Jones, lovely to see you.' and I'd get, 'Thank you, but is *Mrs* Saphan here? If you don't mind, I'd like to talk to her. Or, 'Hannah is such a good listener – not that you're not of course – but...' Then there was the twice weekly pensioner's tea and biscuits, 'Oh, Mrs Saphan doesn't do it like that, if you don't mind.'

Hannah also helped out with lifts to and from the hospital, so we bought a secondhand, but nice, Y reg, VW golf. But it was always 'I'll just take your car, there's so much more room in it for people to stretch their legs. You don't mind do you, and they do love to see it and talk about old times. There's my keys if you need to go anywhere.'

My car was a classic 1948 Wolseley 14/60 and had taken a lot of time and effort both to find and restore, but of course, it had more room for stiff old legs, so she *had* to use that. Sometimes the elderly can be a little awkward, 'Sorry, the zimmer frame caught the door, it's hardly noticeable.' *Hardly noticeable!* It was a gouge, a crater, the grand canyon etched in steel! If I complained, then it was, 'Surely it's an acceptable sacrifice in the Lord's service.'

Hannah loved investigating different cultures, and the healing rituals that were adopted. She spent time regularly visiting various churches, mosques and day centres. Perhaps too much time, as it did seem to take a lot out of her. On her return after these visits she always looked pale and tired.

'Perhaps you should study medicine?' I said to her once, 'Oh, I do – from all over the world.' she told me, but I already knew that.

'No,' I said, 'I didn't mean that, I meant to be a doctor, go to the university and get properly qualified.'

'Don't be silly, I'd never get in, I don't have any of the right exam results, besides, that would be so limiting. There is so much more to healing, that modern medicine doesn't understand.'

That's when, besides telling me all about the different cultures and their methods, she first mentioned reiki, 'It's an area I've a special interest in,' she went on, 'that I feel the church would benefit from because of its nature, and its emphasis on spiritual healing.'

There was a practitioner that she knew that she wanted me to meet with. I went along with it for her sake. Also I thought: *if she has interests of her own to follow, then perhaps she'll be less intrusive of mine.* Yes, I know. I admit it. I am not the perfect minister of God that you, perhaps, thought I was. I am subject to selfish motives, just as the rest of us are.

We went together. When we arrived, I was introduced to a middle aged man, whose fringe was receding and trying to become his bald spot, and he had eyebrows so long they looked to be trying to compensate. He was tall, fairly thin and angular looking, but when he spoke he made you feel warm. There was no other way of putting it. His words swum over one like a warm bath. He could have been reading the dictionary and would have achieved the same effect. 'Welcome to my offices, Pastor, Mrs Saphan. Come in, come in. How much has Hannah told you already?'

'I'm Ben. No need for the pastor or titles, just Ben.'

'Thank you, I'm William. I have been practicing reiki for a number of years now. And have been helping Hannah, for quite a while.'

I was surprised, 'Quite a while?'

'Yes,' said Hannah, 'I've been coming here regularly.'

'It is a non religious philosophy that we hold to.'

'Secular? I'm sorry – I am a man of God. Hannah, you know this. What did you bring me for?'

'Please don't misunderstand,' that calming voice, 'when I say non religious, I mean not affiliated to a church or particular faith – but nonetheless reliant upon a spiritual understanding, as, I believe, is a fair chunk of the Bible."

I wasn't too sure about that, but said nothing.

Hannah said 'Please Ben, just hear it out.'

William then explained the beginnings of reiki during the latter part of the nineteenth century, 'The techniques were developed by a man called Mikao Usui after years of medita-tion. The word reiki is made of two Japanese words - rei which means "God's Wisdom or the Higher Power" and ki which is "life force energy". So reiki is actually "spiritually guided life force energy." In its simplest form a practitioner runs their hands just above, or gently touching a patient's body, helping to reduce stress and promote healing by encouraging a healthy flow of life force energy. It helps with relaxation, anxiety, pain management, and depression.'

'And the spiritual wellbeing of the individual,' Hannah added.

'Yes and the improved mental health affects the physical health too.'

William, Mr Fillips, continued to explain that to become and remain a teacher, one had simply to attend sessions and read the books to attain an understanding. He himself still attended reiki sessions with his mentor and would continue to do so.

'Does anyone ever actually find a cure, for whatever?' I asked.

'Excellent question.' William went on to say 'We have had many successes, both spiritually and physically.' He sounded like a talking brochure.

Me again, 'How does God come into it?'

'I am not a member of the church, but I have my own faith,' said William, 'I believe all life is linked and we as spiritual beings are inspired, both by nature and each other. If one believes that those things are in turn inspired by God, as you say, then Mikao Usui himself must have been so inspired.'

I gave the matter a lot of thought and finally, when I reasoned that God must indeed have been the inspiration behind it all, I surmised that therefore patients could learn from reiki some of the same things that they learned in church about living a spiritual life. I embraced reiki with an open mind, if not quite the enthusiasm of Hannah. She now told me that she had been taking reiki classes since she could remember, almost at her mother's knee, and had been a reiki master for a few years. It was a simple technique to learn and pass on. Wherever she had been, she had given classes. Many reported some almost miraculous results. Now, she informed me, she wanted to set up a clinic where we lived.

She said to me 'We will have to have some rooms for the clinic.'

That was the first stumbling block. I told her 'We have a garage and a spare room, or I suppose we could always convert the front parlour, as we hardly use it for anything anyway.' She didn't think that would be particularly professional. Of course not, it had been my idea.

'No, we will have to find somewhere more suitable.'

In the end we did find somewhere. It was a bit nearer to the hustle and bustle of life and it was relatively cheap. It was a run down building previously used as a hostel in Anerley. As long as we renovated it ourselves, then we could use it for a nominal rent. We reached into our coffers and found the money to pay a friend of a friend to do the necessary work, and opened the Anerley Wellness Centre.

At first we continued the work of the church there: counselling sessions, bible classes, and a drop in centre for spiritual awareness. That is, until Hannah became confident enough in all around her to start reiki sessions. From then on we held the sessions regularly, by appointment only. They proved popular, but we weren't overwhelmed, mainly, I thought, because we had to charge per session to cover costs. Hannah also insisted on taking Wednesdays away, 'To recover,' she said, with no other explanation.

Extraordinarily, it worked. I mean, people were helped. She was a natural teacher. After a series of treatments people said they moved easier, their aches and pains were lessened, and they felt mentally lighter. Appointments grew, I took to learning reiki myself and we took on a masseuse. The centre expanded as we 'did up' a couple more of the rooms. This all took up time and we became a bit like ships passing in the night.

I would promote her sessions at the clinic through the notices at the end of the church services and, though at first people treated it as some sort of spiritual spa day which wasn't cheap, our client list grew.

My concern was that Hannah should take more care day to day and I couldn't understand how someone so caring could be so accident prone; she always seemed to have some injury to patch up, from broken glass to scissors slipping, catching her finger in a drawer, and on and on.

At the clinic occasionally there were some great successes and someone would be healed.

'I've had this condition for years, and I've tried all sorts. The Anerley wellness centre made a huge difference.'

'A couple of sessions here, which I may say were very pleasant and relaxing, and it's gone.'

'I can hardly believe it. It's changed my life'

— QUOTES FROM THE LOCAL PAPER.

Once, after a particularly startling healing where a woman who suffered with both COPD and migraines had been cured apparently instantly. Actually it had taken a number of sessions, but that didn't lessen the effect, although it did sensationalise it and sell a few more newspapers.

I knew that reiki was not a religion and there was nothing you had to believe in order to learn and use it. But I convinced myself that as reiki comes from God, many people could use it to put them more in touch with the experience of their religion rather than having only an intellectual concept of it. This was an aspect that was heavily promoted. In fact, its promotion was a condition of having the clinic at all. I had insisted that the clinic was associated with the church, and that any benefits through it were to be considered the work of God. As I was God's representative in the parish, then the church should take credit for any and all 'miracles.'

I did agree that Mikao Usui's principles should be followed; in that one should practice ethical ideals to promote peace and harmony, and to improve oneself. In a frame on the wall at the entrance to the clinic were these words.

The secret art of inviting happiness,
The miraculous medicine of all diseases.
Just for today, do not anger
Do not worry and be filled with gratitude
Devote yourself to your work. Be kind to people.
Every morning and evening, join your hands in prayer.
Pray these words with your heart
and chant these words with your mouth.
Usui Reiki Treatment for the improvement of body and mind.
The founder, Usui Mikao

Following the newspaper articles the clinic became hugely successful. Despite the high cost, bookings for the sessions were always filled immediately. Local people became interested, applied, and were trained to become reiki teachers. Then the premises had to be expanded to cope with the greater number of classes and clients. Over time, there were many more successes. To a degree I, the church, the reiki centre, which now became The Wellness Centre, and Hannah, thrived. Until the fire.

Hannah also helped out in the church by handing out orders of service at weddings and funerals. Slowly, and I don't really know how it happened, perhaps because I let it, she began to exert a sort of control over things. She was never in charge, per se, but she became the hub around which the church functioned. Her way, always her way. I stopped talking about my plans and ideas, because they were always inappropriate, or at least she knew a better way of doing things. I lost confidence and, for an escape – a chance to be myself again – I started going out and meeting up with a few old friends; for a drink and a chat, nothing major. Maybe I began to enjoy that too much and, to be honest, I did really look forward to it. It was my 'me' time. The downside of this was that I became very frustrated and occasionally, but only when I'd had a drink, my frustration boiled over. I never did resort to actual violence, although I think I may have been forgiven if I had.

Then Rachel was born. I couldn't believe it. The doctors had been wrong, so wrong. I was still in my prime. I still had plenty of appetite, and health seemed to be my middle name. During that time, I can't remember even catching a cold.

⁓

Hannah's sister, Abigail, turned up on the doorstep one day, homeless. I didn't even know she had a sister. She was younger and, to be kind, she was a little too flirtatious for my liking; but she moved in 'temporarily'. I continuously asked her to dress herself properly, but she didn't seem to care. Even in the house she would walk about in her underwear; oblivious, provocative. She seemed to be in every room I entered. She was untidy and helped very little with the housework. It was the cause of more than one argument with Hannah.

To be fair, she did get a part time job and paid something toward her keep. I asked Hannah. 'How long is she going to be here, I really don't think it's a good thing for us, or the church's reputation, the way she behaves.'

But she was adamant, 'She is my sister, she has had to put up with a lot in her life and, besides, she has nowhere else to go.' And when I asked about her extended family, and whether she could stay with them for a while, 'How can you speak of another human being like that? Show some of your charity. Her life is here, not up in the wilds of Yorkshire. Stop thinking of yourself so much – Or are you thinking of her too much? Is that it?'

I'm sorry to say, I stormed out. Slamming as many doors as I could through the house. Giving entirely the wrong impression of how I felt. *How dare she? I am a man of God!* However, I am still a man, and perhaps there was a little in what she said.

After that I tried to avoid seeing so much of Abigail. I retreated into my study for much of the time. There was a mention of some man she was seeing and then, abruptly, she did go away; I don't know why. When she eventually came back, she was different.

We had been married for just over five years, and fallen into a routine. Hannah ran the centre, which had a regular clientele, and helped with the outreach programme, including the pensioner's tea and cake afternoons. I ran the church, did the hospital and home visits. The healing services were a very important part of the churches work and were well attended.

I popped into the centre every now and then for my own sessions – though not from Hannah. We regularly invited outside practitioners to come in and use our space. Occasionally Hannah would help out at the church healing services, especially when we were a helper short. It was during one of those services that it happened.

It was an accident really. I had called the supplicants to the front of the church and onto the wide chancel, a semi circular, raised stage around the altar. As Peter Brook might have called it, *The Empty Space*, it was where the theatre happened. I was busy casting out demons from a particular young man and calling, 'Lord we ask that you show your infinite mercy and lift this burden from him, in the name of Jesus. Amen.' Then I pushed against his forehead, perhaps a little too enthusiastically, and, due to the young man's balance being impaired by his condition, he fell from the edge of the stage. It was only a matter of a few inches, but he landed awkwardly and banged his head on the front pew, causing a small cut, which being on his head, bled profusely.

As fortune would have it, Hannah was behind him as he tumbled, taking most of his weight. Otherwise he may have suffered a great deal more than just a small cut; but she was carried by his momentum into the same pew and, in trying to save them, grabbed at – anything, caught her nail and tore it off. She screamed, blood welled up from her finger, but she held tight to protect the young man's head. There was confusion, a fuss where everyone rushed forward to help, or to see what was going on. She had blacked out.

'Hannah?' I said softly, kneeling over her. 'Hannah, can you hear me?'

She opened her eyes. 'Thank the Lord!' I sighed with relief, 'Come and sit down. Move back please, let them both breathe.'

'Call an ambulance, somebody.' Mobile phones were switched on and people dialled 999 all at the same time. 'One, please. Just one of you.'

Well-meaning people were fussing around, over they knew not what, but wanted to be included in the excitement. In short, there was pandemonium. When all had calmed down, and everyone was assured there was no major damage, a way was cleared and both the young man and Hannah were escorted to the vestry to clean up. Blood seemed to be all over them, from his head wound and Hannah's finger; there was no knowing whose blood was whose.

Shortly thereafter, the ambulance arrived. 'They may seem minor injuries,' said the paramedic to Hannah, 'but you were unconscious for a little while and you, George, banged your head too. We think it's only prudent that you should both come to the hospital to check you over.'

'Is it really necessary ?' said a woman from the congregation, 'We have a very important birthday lunch to get to. Is my husband seriously hurt?'

'I'm sorry, it is the best thing. One never knows with head injuries. You can come with us if you'd like.'

'Oh, I will, George hasn't been well lately you know. He's been under the doctor, I can help explain things.'

'Ben,' said Hannah quietly, 'I really don't need to go to the hospital, I can patch up my finger, I'll be fine.'

The paramedic overheard. 'I'm sorry, I believe you were unconscious for a short while. We can't take any chances. Just a quick check up and you'll be home in no time.'

'If you must,' said Hannah resignedly.

'Right you are then.'

The two paramedics supervised the journey out to the ambulance and, after making sure that both Hannah and George were comfortable and secure – and Mrs Roven was unhappily holding her husband's hand, one climbed into the cab while the other closed the doors.

'I'll call the hospital just as soon as I clean up here!' I called, as the ambulance doors closed and it drove slowly away. I turned to sort out the mess. As I went back inside, I was pressed on all sides. 'Is Mrs Saphan alright?'

'What a lovely woman she is.'

'Things like that always happen to the best of us.'

'Weren't you supposed to be healing people?'

'Is there anything I can do until Mrs Saphan gets well?'

'She's not ill!' A little sharper than I would have liked, 'She's simply cut her hand.'

'And she had a bad fall.'

'Knocked her clean out. She was only helping that man.'

I was silently seething, but with a smile locked in place. The service had been made a mockery of. Respect had disappeared. Instead of healing, someone had been hurt and these people were walking across the chancel as if it were a zebra crossing. Not only that but there had been no collection plate, and there had been a sizeable congregation for a change. *Oh, yes, they all loved her.*

When everyone had left, I went into the vestry, picked up a glass, and filled it from a communion wine bottle. *It hasn't been blessed yet anyway.* I drank it in one, then refilled it, paused, then threw the glass and its contents hard against the wall. I hated the way I felt. I was a servant of God! 'Shit!'

Hannah came home in a taxi. I offloaded onto her, 'I couldn't sit at the hospital for who knows how long. I've got far too much to do. More,' pointing at her damaged hand, 'now that you've done that! – Your sister is no help at all either. Off all night.'

From seemingly nowhere, a rage had come over me.

'That service was ruined. Do you really understand what it means. Really?' I literally saw red.

Hannah was lost for words. What had she done? A difficult evening followed. I drank some more; I couldn't think how else to calm down, to escape my fury. I may have said some things I now regret. The next day, Hannah found it difficult to look people in the eye.

A few days later the house phone rang. *Yet another parishioner, wanting her,* I thought, then immediately, *Why shouldn't they? She's my wife after all. The pastor's wife.*

I picked up the receiver. 'Mornin'. The Herald here, am I speaking to Pastor Saphan?'

'Er – yes, speaking. Who is this?'

'Peter Davis, The Herald. Could I ask you to comment on a story we're about to run?'

'Ye-es, if it's a story I can comment on.'

'Good, erm a man by the name of ...'

There was the sound of rustling paper. 'George Roven, is saying that there has been some kind of a miracle. He came to your service, er, healing service, and he's – well – healed!'

'I beg your pardon! Who?'

'Roven, George Roven. He said there had been an accident and that when he got to the hospital, he'd been cured.'

'Yes, there was an unfortunate…'. I was thinking fast, "I will certainly be speaking, er – and praying with him, to see if God has truly worked a miracle through my ministry. How is he after the acci – oh, of course, sorry.' I started to recover. 'The church has always been a vessel for the power of God and if He has chosen to bless us this way, then that is forever to His glory and our debt.'

'Thank you Mr Saphan.'

'Pastor Saphan.' I hung up.

'Hannah!' I shouted to her as I pulled on my coat, 'Who the hell is this George Roven? Where does he live?'

George Roven had arrived at the hospital with Hannah and, after several hours, had finally seen a doctor. He had been complaining of the pain in his head after his fall, so as a precaution he was sent for a CT scan. Fortunately it showed no damage, but what it did show was the tumour. It had been there a while, and was the cause of him losing his balance occasionally. Along with slurring his words, it gave people the impression that he had been drinking whereas, in fact, George was teetotal. The thing about this scan was that, when compared to a previous one, the tumour seemed to have shrunk. Subsequent scans and consultations within the hospital over the next few days showed it had shrunk further and finally blood tests proved that it was no longer a threat to him as it had become benign.

I found Mr Roven, who was overjoyed. *Who wouldn't be if they'd just had their death sentence overturned.* Mrs Roven couldn't understand the difference in him.

'He's got so much energy. It's like he's on drugs. He's not though – only what the doctors give him, but he won't take them anyway – says he doesn't need them any more!'

I prayed with him, told him that it was God's will that he'd been cured, and it was indeed a miracle. Then I shouted it from the rooftops. At every opportunity. I was euphoric. Here in this church, this ministry, God had chosen to show Himself. Through me!

Word spread like wildfire. The church was full to capacity at every service and, when called forward for the healing service, numbers had to be restricted to only the worst cases; now there were larger, burlier helpers on hand to make sure that that was the case. God had surely blessed this church.

Hannah's hand healed well and she carried on with her duties as before; now all anybody wanted to do was to speak to the Pastor, or touch me as if I had some magical properties that would rub off. Though inconvenient at times, that did feel good.

The hospital called, could Mrs Saphan attend the phlebotomy clinic? She was a bit hesitant, but we made an appointment. I put it down to her not liking needles being stuck in her. Understandable.

On the day I drove Hannah to the appointment. Following the church incident, Hannah had had her bloods checked, as a matter of precaution and for the record, as they didn't seem to have her on their database. They wanted to take another sample to check against the first. 'Just routine,' they said.

'Mrs Saphan, has anybody ever mentioned anything to you that suggests any abnormalities?'

'No, I don't think so. I do regularly give blood. There's never been a problem if that's the sort of thing.'

'When was the last time you were poorly?'

'I don't remember, it must have been a while ago, probably a cold or something. I don't get ill very often, I am very careful about hygiene.'

'That's very good, we should all think about that. But – really ill – bed ridden? Nothing like that?'

'Oh, I don't think so. Not since being a child.'

'You were ill as a child?'

'Why?'

'Well, we found something about your blood. Nothing to worry about, nothing wrong at all, just sort of – different.'

'What sort of thing?' Hannah had had this conversation before. She gave blood regularly, quietly, in different places under different names. Perhaps too regularly, accounting for her complexion. She was usually so careful.

'We don't know, that's why we thought we'd ask you to come in. Could you roll up your sleeve please? The right one?'

Hannah drew her arm away from the needle. 'No, not just now, I am feeling a little under the weather – now that you mention it – and I'd like to go home please.'

'Of course, but it would only take a moment, then you can be off.'

'No!'

A little more forcefully. 'I am going home. Thank you'

'But Mrs Saphan – '

'There's nothing wrong with my blood, you probably contaminated it. I did notice the stress this hospital was under, and I'm not surprised that mistakes are made. I'm not prepared to supply you with endless samples to cover your incompetence.'

She got up and marched out of the room, followed by the phlebotomist protesting, "But…"

She hated behaving like this, but in the long run it was best. I was just nodding off in a chair outside the room and heard the commotion; as Hannah passed me I was brusquely poked awake and I hurried behind Hannah in utter bemusement.

~

'What in God's name was that all about?'

'Nothing, the hospital made a mistake. That's all. It's nothing.'

'It sounds like you know all about this nothing. What's going on?' I was getting upset now.

'I promise you, there's nothing going on. They made a mistake with the blood. That's all.' Hannah had known this would happen. She looked across at Abigail for help.

'Don't look at me. Tell him. He's your husband'

I was confused. 'Tell me what? Are you ill?'

'No – no, honestly, there's nothing like that.'

I was shouting now. 'Then what in heaven is it. Tell me. Now!'

Silence.

'Have you ever looked up your family tree?'

'Oh, for goodness sake,' said Abigail, 'I'm going to make some tea. This could take a while.'

'You want to know? Then I'll tell you. All of it Abigail – from the beginning. We have a family tree. It stretches way back. I didn't look it up or research it. I didn't have to. My family have kept very careful records for centuries.'

'That's all very well and nice. Good for you, but what is this business about the blood?' I found it very hard to be patient.

'In good time,' said Hannah keeping calm. 'You know your Bible, but do you know the book of Tobit?'

'No,' I said 'There isn't a book of Tobit.'

'It is a historical text from somewhere around 300 BCE – not included in the Bible. It's in the Apocrypha. It is the book of the words of Tobit, son of Tobiel, the son of Ananiel, the son of Aduel, the son of Gabael, of the seed of Asael, of the tribe of Nephthali – '

'I've never come across – '

'There is a story within it that refers to the angel Raphael.'

She continued, 'A woman of great beauty, with child, called Adah was working in a field near a town called Ecbatana when she found a child dying of starvation at the side of the pathway. She had no means of helping the child, save suckling and allowing the child of her own milk. The child revived and Adah nursed it as her own. The angel Raphael was watching and felt love for Adah and knew her and imparted his vitality into her. He promised her that for her sacrifice his gift would live in her and in the firstborn of her firstborn for eternity; that her descendants would share the gift of her life's blood, and would heal and be healed by it.'

'And you're going to tell me that she was your great grand-mother?' I laughed stupidly.

'Essentially – yes. The family records have been kept since that was written, and every firstborn child inherits her blood. Her life's blood that heals.'

'Just to be clear, you are the oldest, you are the firstborn in your family?'

Quietly, seriously, she said 'Yes.'

Abigail returned with a teapot, milk, and cups. She set them on the table.

'I think I want something a little stronger than that,' I said almost to myself, 'And does that mean, our firstborn, Elliot?'

'Yes,' said Hannah. 'Elliot is our firstborn – as he matures his blood will exhibit the same properties.'

'What about Rachel?'

'No, not Rachel,' she shook her head.

'Oh no, never the second child,' said Abigail

'And your family has kept this secret all that time,' I pressed on. 'Not shared it with anyone?'

'It has become known from time to time – with consequences. Some have been tried as witches, others crushed or cut to pieces by mobs who wanted to benefit themselves. So I keep it to myself, as I have been taught. But I give blood as often as my body will allow, and it goes randomly into the world helping any who receive it. And in that way I share as much as I can with others.'

Hannah sat down to pour the tea. She was watching me. 'It's so important that you understand Ben.'

Oh, I understood. Now she'd even taken away *my* miracle.

'This is a gift from Raphael you said?'

'Yes – so it says in the writings,' Hannah replied.

'So, it doesn't come from God?'

'Of course it does Ben, what are you saying?'

'It's a story from some apocryphal writing about an angel that raped a woman.'

'No,' said Hannah

'And *this* then is something we must honour?' I just wanted to hurt her.

'No Ben – please understand.'

'And what about you Abigail?' I turned to look at Abigail.

'Oh, no!' said Abigail, 'I've never met any angels. Everything I touch turns into a bloody disaster – like all my relationships.'

'So, this business with whatshisname, Rodent?'

'George Roven.'

'Yes. George Roven. You cured his tumour?'

'Yes. Well not me, but something in my blood. That's what the hospitals were talking about. There is nothing detectable, nothing extra in my blood, but it has a sort of energy – an invisible glow. It must have got into Mr Roven when both of us suffered blood injuries, and they mixed together in the cut on his head.'

'And the little "accidents" that you keep having?'

'You're right Ben – they're not accidents. I take a droplet sometimes to help alleviate somebody's suffering.'

'For *your* own glory and pride and benefit. All the things we are taught not to encourage!'

Abigail chipped in 'It seems to work like the exact opposite of HIV. That's why you never catch cold Ben.'

Hannah blushed. 'Yes, it pretty much works in the same way too, passing to another through bodily fluids, not just through the blood.'

'And sex, so, as they say, plenty is good for you,' said Abigail looking from one to the other of us. 'Well, isn't it?'

'Yes,' said Hannah, 'It works that way too.'

'Not any more.' I left the room.

The greater good. That's a big thing, morally speaking. Should one hurt someone else, or steal from them, or inconvenience them in some way – if it will benefit others? It would need to be lots of others, otherwise it's just choosing one person over another. Is it morally right? This story about angels and magic blood. *Could it be true?* The evidence of George whatshisname, seems to confirm it. If it is true: then can it be used, for the greater good? Can it be used in a more targeted fashion through the church and the Glory of God?

Getting hold of some of this life giving liquid may prove awkward though. One cannot simply approach someone (Hannah) and say 'Excuse me, could I have a pint of your blood?' She would never agree to it. It may produce a variety of reactions. So how? It must be done unknowingly, asleep: the need for something sleep inducing is apparent.

An ordinary, non medical, person cannot go and buy prescriptive drugs over the counter; so one has to make some enquiries. After a little research I found that a drug called Flunitrazepam is perfect. I'm told that some call it 'roofies' or 'loonies' and it's sold, if not openly – certainly legally, as rohypnol. This apparently can cause sleep within ten to fifteen minutes, with few after effects.

One of the benefits of being a minister in the church is that people talk to me, quite frankly, about things that they may not normally feel that they could talk about. It's the immunity thing, everything is 'in confidence'. A priest never talks, that kind of thing. As a result of that, I had come to know people from all walks of life. One or two discreet enquiries and I had obtained some of the aforementioned drug. Simple little capsules. They were in my pocket.

I'd had nothing to eat, but it wasn't food that I needed. It was something else, I needed solace. Courage? I needed a drink. Not alone, one should never drink alone, but with a couple of friends who didn't ask what was wrong, didn't offer a shoulder to cry on, or any old wives homilies; just something to drink and forget with. I made a call and arranged to meet up with a couple of old friends. I hadn't intended to stay too long but, well you know what it's like. We laughed about the anomalies of life. The more we drank, the more we laughed. We farted, we swore, we were in a safe place. Well, safe from anyone else. The evening turned into night, I was tired. It was time I got back. It was quite a walk too, but I got there. I don't know what the time was but there were no lights on. I opened the door. Immediately, the light went on upstairs, she had obviously been waiting. *Here we go!* I met her head on at the bottom of the stairs.

'I'm glad you're back.'

'Can't I go out with my friends? Do I need your permission for that? You can swan off with your precious therapist can't you? You think I don't know? When was the last time he was ill, eh? Is that what you call *therapy*?'

'No Ben – it's not that. I'm sorry.'

'Oh, I see. Sorry are you, it's a bit late for sorry now isn't it. You've ruined it between us. My church, My faith. You've taken it all!'

'Ben,' she said 'Ben, shhh, the children. I'm not putting up with this.' She went up the stairs, I followed.

'*You're* not putting up with it. *You!*' It was all coming out. I couldn't stop.

'Your children – even that wasn't me was it?' I was getting louder, more confident. 'It was you and your magic blood. Everything's *you*, you've made me nothing. You're a witch!'

'Ben please, we'll talk in the morning.'

'I'm still the man here. You're my wife,' I walked forward, she had to back away, she looked scared. *Good, it serves her right for once.*

'No, Ben. Not now, not like this!' she pleaded. She backed into the kids' bedroom.

'Sex? I don't want sex with you.'

The large solid built wardrobe was right behind her, with the door wide open, she stumbled and tripped backwards; though she didn't fall, she finished up inside it. I fished a capsule out of my pocket and forced it into her mouth. She swallowed. I shut the door. And pushed the bolt across.

'No. Ben open the door.' The kids didn't stir.

I didn't answer, and went downstairs. I sat at the kitchen table. The clock ticked on.

About ten minutes later it all went quiet upstairs. I had to improvise. I went to the drawer and got the very sharp knife. The one we always knew was the sharp one; for cutting onions and such. I gave it a careful wipe and took it with a small resealable cup upstairs. Hannah was fast asleep. Unwakeable. I took what I wanted from her arm and went back down into my study. I opened a bottle of the communion wine I kept there, had a good drink of it, and then emptied the cup into it. I took it back to the kitchen and put the bottle into the fridge.

It was very late. The energy of bonhomie had gone now, replaced by heaviness. The front door opened, I heard it but didn't care.

'What the – ? Abigail?'

She came into the kitchen, half dressed as usual – well she looked it. She leant over me, 'What are you doing here?'

'It's alright Ben, just relax.'

I reached out, her breast was there, under my hand.

She smiled, but didn't pull away, then she threw her head back and laughed; as she did so her top came partly open, and I saw Eden. I reached again, this time deliberately, and held her other breast. I moved to kiss her; this time she reacted.

'Get off me, you pervert. My sister is upstairs. If you want that, go there.' She pushed me and I sat down again. Somehow my hand connected with her head, not on purpose, but hard. I tried a sneer anyway. She swore at me as tears formed in her eyes. She looked about and crossed the room; then opened the icebox in the fridge, picked up a bag of frozen peas, and held them to her face. She paused as if about to say something else, thought better of it, and stormed out of the house.

What had I done? It was Hannah's fault; all that blood business and it had been so long since I'd gone near her. Then *she* had to come back, flaunting herself. Who can blame me for trying? But I knew the answer to that. My head felt heavy. I dropped it onto my hands. Too hard. It banged on the table, but it didn't hurt.

If I just closed my eyes, it would be all right. I'll wake up and it will all be as it always was. But it wouldn't. I wanted to feel good. *Couldn't she give me that?* The words were slightly slurred. 'She is not God.' I was hungry.

'Toast. I must have something.' There wasn't even anything left out. I raised myself and fumbled in the dark kitchen, found a loaf in the cupboard and a tin of something, it looked like beans. 'Whoops, steady,' as I lost my balance for a second. I steadied myself, switched the cooker on at the grill and slid the bread under. 'Butter.' The table was between me and the fridge. It was slipping sideways. I lunged for it, but banged my thigh on the straight backed wooden chair in the way.

'Shh!' I hissed to nobody, rubbed my leg, then a coughing spasm took me for a moment, 'She wouldn't hear it anyway.' I was pleased with myself, it was my turn to laugh. I remembered the toast. 'I don't want 'ny butter.' A long cheek puffing sigh relaxed me, and I sat down again. 'Nah!'

There were loud noises from upstairs which caught my attention for a moment. 'Yeah, that's right. Bang, bang. I know! When I'm ready!' The room was spinning. I closed my eyes but that only made it worse. They were so heavy, so heavy. This time I rested more gently on the table and relaxed.

Why couldn't they just leave me be? Alright, I'd come home later than I thought I would. I may even have been a little loud, but who wouldn't, after a few glasses of whisky. What else would you do in the company of a few encouraging fellows? How dare she speak to me in that way. In my house. She was better was she? How much time had passed, it seemed like forever. I stood up, a sudden energising burst of anger took me. Out into the hallway and upstairs.

She always put the kids first. 'Why you?' I'd screamed. 'I'm the one it should be! I've given my life. You! You've done nothing.'

She was concerned about the kids? Then let her be with the kids. All bloody night, for all I cared. There was no reply from inside.

'Oh it's that game now is it? Well, please yourself then.' What was she doing in there? I went in, the door to the wardrobe was open, I was sure I'd bolted it.

'You can be as quiet as you like. You're not coming out.' I stage whispered, so as not to wake the children. I slowly backed out of the room, turned the doorknob and locked it. I removed the key from the lock and put it in my pocket. Now she'll have to wait for the morning.

'Your sister lives in our house and she's nice to everyone else. Well, it's about time she was nice to me too.'

I almost slipped on the stairs going down, 'Whoops, careful!' and back into the kitchen. I opened the cutlery drawer and found the tin opener. It wouldn't fit on the rim of the tin. I sat down again. 'So tired. Huh – serve her right,' I heard myself say, 'Just for a while,' as I slipped into drowsiness and then sleep. At some time, maybe in a dream, perhaps I thought I heard the banging as the door closed. I drooled a smile.

I awoke coughing, there was a roaring in my ears, my head felt it was was splitting apart. The room was dark, and foggy, and hot. No – not foggy, smoke! The toast!

It was too late for toast, that had burned hours ago and set light to the paper towels beneath it as pieces had fallen off. I looked around in horror. That must have lit the curtains; and flames had leapt up and consumed the entire ceiling. I staggered from the room, trying to catch my breath, to the base of the stairs. She was in the bedroom above the kitchen. *Oh God! I locked the door!* Where was that bloody key? I threw my jacket over my head and forced my legs to work as best they could up the stairs, to be met by a small screaming figure coming down.

It was on fire, or part of it was. The boy had forced his way through the burning door. *Where were his mother and sister? Still in the choking, smoke filled bedroom?* It was too hot, there wasn't time. I couldn't think. There was no point anyway. It was too late. Staggering backwards, losing my balance, I grabbed at something, caught a t-shirt, stumbled back down the stairs and out of the front door. I tried, with my own jacket, to smother and beat the flaming flesh of the small screaming figure that I'd dragged along.

Sirens were approaching, someone must have called them. *Too late!* I became aware of people all around me, someone took the child. God it was cold! I thrust my hands into my pockets to keep them warm, and felt something hard. *The key.* Slowly my mind caught up. No – no – no! A way out. Escape. I needed to try to go back into the house.

'My wife!' I shouted, 'My daughter.'

A voice shouted back, 'You saved your son, there's no more you can do. You've done enough.'

Only I knew that I had not. I shrugged the helping hands aside and made a dash for the door. It was still open. My god, the heat! The fire had not yet descended the stairs; once inside I threw the key upstairs as hard as I could and turned to the kitchen to get the bottle as the arms once again encircled me and forced me outside.

I sat in the hospital and cried. For Hannah, for Rachel, for little Elliot's hands – but mostly for me. I had done this. They were talking about me being a hero. *Not me.* I had let them all down, and I had let God down. I was shit, garbage, blood on the floor, to be got rid of as quickly and quietly as possible. People had wanted to shake my hand, even as the ambulance doors closed. Here I sat in a small room, alone. Unhurt. However, I wasn't alone, I still had Elliot, little Elliot, all I had left of my family, and even he was damaged.

I had to pull myself together, if only for his sake. I had nowhere to live. I'm sure the church will help there, I'll speak to the counsellor person here and try to organise something. I was about to stand when I looked toward the door, which was still half open; I hadn't noticed. That was Abigail.

'Abigail!' I called.

She stopped and came in. She opened her arms wide to hold

me, to offer me comfort. But even now, even with all that was going on, all I saw was woman and I felt her warmth as her arms held me. I told her about Hannah, and Rachel. I tried to tell her what had happened, with as much truth as I could accept. She bore it very well. Just then someone in a uniform came in and said the consultant wanted to see me. We both went. We were offered comfort but also facts. Elliot would need a lot of care and many visits to the hospital and he may never recover full use of his hands.

Abigail went off to try and find her friend while I asked about the counsellor person. Before I had time to go looking though, Abigail came back with a look of desperation on her face.

'Ben. I've got nowhere to live – I can't stay in hotels – can I stay with you for a while? Just until I get sorted out.'

I knew the church was obliged to find me something and, of course, Elliot, but I didn't know about anything beyond that. 'I'll try, if you really haven't got anywhere else. If I do, it will only be temporary.'

In the end, it worked out very conveniently. The elders found us a flat within a short walk of the church and, as it was a two bed flat, Abigail could stay too. Every time I went to the church, which was practically every day, I was faced with what was left of the house right next door, faced with the stark reality of the consequences of my actions. That is until they eventually demolished it and sold the land off to a builder.

I was relieved of a great deal of trouble dealing with child care for Elliot and was provided a live-in housekeeper, Abigail, too. My car had, miraculously, survived the fire but there was nowhere at the flat to park it. I had to find a lock up to put it in. After all it was an extremely rare example of a valuable classic car. Apart from that, the arrangement worked very well for us all. Although Abigail did seem to have changed and become a more demure person; in personality and dress sense. Her presence still affected me, and I could not shake that picture of her from my mind. I am ashamed to say that on occasion I had to shut myself in the bathroom to deal with it.

She kept herself to herself as much as she could. Possibly through guilt, or consideration, or even gratitude. Perhaps her life was filled up with Elliot's needs. It meant that sometimes I even forgot she was there. Late one evening, she had gone to bed and I was in the bathroom, she came in. She obviously wasn't expecting me to be there, and certainly not engaging in any such activity. She had suddenly needed the loo. I hadn't locked the door. We both froze! She burst out laughing at the incongruity of our situation and immediately flooded the floor. She was shocked, at herself in truth, not me, and I was shocked and embarrassed all at once. We looked at each other.

'This is no good Ben. We can't go pussy footing around each other like this. I'm not blind or daft. We are both adults. Even though you are a pastor and should probably know better.'

'No, I'm sorry,' I said, belatedly scrabbling at my clothes. 'I'll get on to the elders in the morning. I'll tell them it's not working and we'll find somewhere for you. I am so sorry.'

'That's not what I mean,' she said. 'This may sound – unusual, but I am grateful and very happy living here. I don't want to leave. If it would help, from time to time, you don't have to hide in the bathroom. Just talk to me. Nothing else, just this.'

I was confused, am I hearing this right, but calmly I said, 'Abi, I do have difficulty with you around, but only because you are a very attractive woman. We seem to manage around one another. That sort of arrangement would – '

'No!' she said suddenly. 'Not an arrangement and not all the time.'

'All right,' I said meekly. 'As you say.'

She nodded and changed the subject. 'Oh dear, what a mess. We need to clean up in here, I'll get the towels.'

I pushed my luck. *Well, while the iron is hot, so to speak.* 'Before that, I'm still – ready. Would you?'

It was only a couple of minutes later that she washed her hands and fetched the paper towels. I didn't think at the time, who does, but that 'conversation' changed things. Suddenly the balance had changed. I found myself questioned over decisions that previously had been taken for granted, agreeing to childcare things that I actually didn't want to do. Abigail became much more like the woman she was before the fire.

Eventually the church elders found a more appropriate living space for us. A property they owned, not nearer to the church but much, much more comfortable, with a gravelled driveway so that I could have my car back and in a safe space. Elliot was growing and he was needing a proper bedroom of his own; this house gave him that.

We were going to have to be careful about managing Elliot, what he knew and what he didn't know. I discussed him with Abigail. He wasn't interested in girls yet. At least there had been no evidence of it, but one day he would be and he would have to know it all. We agreed to keep an eye open for developments.

There were many visits to the hospital for Elliot and quite a few operations. It cut me deeply every time, but I knew I had to suffer for my sin. After the move, Abigail removed her favour. The balance remained. *Was it a plan all along?* I spent more time at the centre now and that was growing slowly, but I did have my own office space at last. All of the paperwork that I had built up had been lost, so there was plenty of room to start again. Start again I did.

Now it's been fifteen years since the fire, and the file cabinets are bulging again. I did move some files from the centre, but there was one I was looking for. I knew it hadn't been destroyed, it must be still there, perhaps it had fallen behind something.

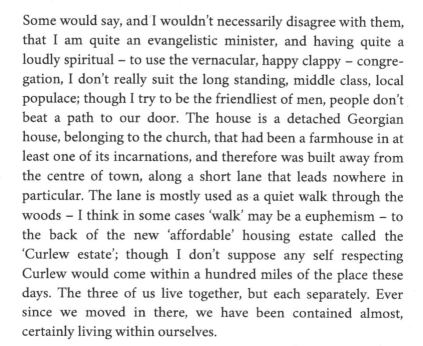

Some would say, and I wouldn't necessarily disagree with them, that I am quite an evangelistic minister, and having quite a loudly spiritual – to use the vernacular, happy clappy – congregation, I don't really suit the long standing, middle class, local populace; though I try to be the friendliest of men, people don't beat a path to our door. The house is a detached Georgian house, belonging to the church, that had been a farmhouse in at least one of its incarnations, and therefore was built away from the centre of town, along a short lane that leads nowhere in particular. The lane is mostly used as a quiet walk through the woods – I think in some cases 'walk' may be a euphemism – to the back of the new 'affordable' housing estate called the 'Curlew estate'; though I don't suppose any self respecting Curlew would come within a hundred miles of the place these days. The three of us live together, but each separately. Ever since we moved in there, we have been contained almost, certainly living within ourselves.

I am sitting in the office at the moment, catching up on a little paper work. Invoices and such. Everything costs so much more these days. Abigail keeps the place nice, cleaning and tidying as she goes, but it's always, 'I'm just going to run the vacuum around, someone's left dirty footprints,' and, 'I'll just wash these pots, shall I?'

Yes, *when I've finished using them!*

It's one thing being clean and tidy. There's a place for everything and, as long as a thing goes into its place, everything fits. But, with Abigail, it's as if every speck of dust or spoon out of place was her mortal enemy and must be immediately vanquished and, by immediately, I mean there isn't time to put things in their proper places. No, they have to go in the nearest available space, out of sight, and by 'washing the pots' what she actually means is putting them in the dishwasher for later, which also means that there aren't any to actually use. If I complain, then 'They're only there, if you want them you can wash them yourself.' I mean, I don't have OCD but constantly having to search cupboards and the dishwasher if I want a bowl and spoon for breakfast is annoying. She never used to be like this. On the contrary, when Hannah was alive Abigail was a most untidy slapdash sort of person. I think I read once that psychologically, if someone is constantly cleaning then they are actually trying to clear, or clean, their mind, turning chaos into some sort of order. But hiding things out of sight might say something else.

I have this office, which I keep the way I like it. I ban everyone from using it, so I know I can find things when I need them. It also gives me a private space to contemplate my navel in peace when necessary. There is a lock on the door, because occasionally I relax by browsing. *Is that a thing?* Abigail may think differently. I do find myself disappearing down internet rabbit holes and, when I re-emerge, an hour or so seems to have passed. I also keep the extra bottles of communion wine in here.

Elliot has turned into an odd fish. He grew up without a mother, but was indulged by his aunt. I didn't agree, 'The world we live in is hard, the sooner the boy learns to cope with it the better.'

She never listened. 'He's just a boy, Ben. There'll be time for all that when he's older. Let him be a boy.'

But Elliot didn't really cope.

'Yes, he's clever enough, but he doesn't connect with people. I'm sure there's something lacking there.'

Abigail insisted, 'He likes his own company, lots of people do.'

I disagreed, 'It's not good for him.'

Elliot was like a puppy. If somebody showed him some kindness, then he thought he had a friend for life and was crushed when it turned out, as it inevitably did, that he didn't. It was that way with girls. A kind word and he thought he was in love and attached himself, like that puppy, only to find out that a smile was just that, a smile, not a declaration of love. Abigail doted on him though, and he could do no wrong. I know young people these days get up to all sorts of things, but Elliot is a worry. He is legally an adult, even though he often doesn't behave as one, and he doesn't have friends that I'm aware of. All that helps, in a way. The wheels of God – and all that. It means that he isn't distracted and can focus on what's important, his work at the church and the centre. The church employs him as an assistant to me and pays him a small wage, which I administer. When he's free he helps out at the Wellness Centre, cleaning and such. While he's there, he also learns about reiki. I think it's important for the future.

His hands started to improve a great deal recently. I hope that helps with his confidence and usefulness. Sometimes I may appear a little hard on him, but it's for his own good. He must learn to work within a group, a team, for the good of others. This requires discipline, which, in turn, needs management.

As a representative of the church, I have to be seen to be an upright, ethical and, if not a pillar, certainly an important member of society and I have to make sure that my staff hold to these standards. I have regular health checks for all staff, including screening for drug use. I know, at least I hope, none of them take recreational drugs, but it's about being seen to be clean and removing any doubt. Since he has become an adult, the same rules apply to Elliot and, for convenience, I take his blood sample at home; I have the equipment locked away in my study.

He is actually doing very well at the centre and it won't be long before he will be competent enough to assist one of our more senior practitioners there. In truth, there are only four of us that work there, including myself, the receptionist, Daisy, and two practitioners. Between us we cover reiki, massage, mental health, and all things in between; all delivered under the spiritual umbrella of God's love. The centre, named after my dear departed wife all those years ago, has been ticking along nicely, managing to pay for itself and building a good reputation over the years.

It all changed recently, and by that I mean over the last couple of years. There have been spiritual energies suddenly apparent among us that have resulted in some of our clients reporting 'miraculous' cures. Nothing so amazing that it makes the news, and not regularly, but small and occasional; such that it has created quite a buzz locally. That in turn has resulted in a greatly increased demand for our services such that I've been using the midweek day off – it's actually changed to Mondays now but we still call it the midweek day off – that we all take to reduce the backlog of enquiries. There are more services at the church now and I don't have time to oversee the centre; so the staff there use that day to go out to visit those who can't get there, through disability or convenience, killing two birds proverbially. Daisy, on reception, takes the day off. That's of course one less expense. However, she does work late most other days and is quite willing to work above and beyond in order to catch up. Win – win for the centre. I have also noticed another interesting benefit of the increased interest and that is a noticeable change in people's attitude toward me personally. The church services are better attended too. Praise be to God.

Elliot is proving himself useful. He went out earlier to fetch me some papers from the centre. They are to do with something I have been working on for a very long time; it's boiling up nicely and I need those papers. I only came across them the other day. I had thought they were lost, but whilst clearing some other papers, they were found stuck behind one of the drawers in the filing cabinet. They must have been there more than oh, fifteen years.

What on earth's going on? I heard the shuddering crash of the door and and chairs scraping over the kitchen floor.

'Is that you Elliot?' I shouted. There was no need, no excuse, for behaviour like this, this was asking for trouble. I was determined that Elliot behave himself properly and I was prepared to make sure he did. Abigail had put down the book she had

BRIAN J. TWIDDY

been enjoying, and came into the kitchen with it still in her hand. I was already there at the bottom of the stairs, furious,

'Elliot, you come back down here now. How dare you treat this house like that. You've got to learn a little respect.'

Abigail said quietly, 'Ben, go easy on him. Something must have happened to upset him.'

'Upset him! I'll give him upset. Elliot! Get down here boy!'

Abigail pushed past me and started up the stairs. 'Just a minute Ben, let me talk to him, find out what's happened.'

'Come down here this minute or I'll be up there – and you know full well what that'll mean.'

Abigail got to the top of the stairs and pushed the bedroom door. It appeared to be locked. 'Elliot?' she called gently, 'Please come down, if there's something the matter we can talk about it.' There was no reply, but there was a muffled sobbing coming from the other side of the door. 'All right love. I'll go back down. Try to calm yourself down – take a few minutes and then join us in the kitchen. Whatever it is, it'll be okay.' Abigail came back down the stairs.

'Whatever it is he's gone and done, it'll be the last time.' I told her. I wasn't aware I was clenching my teeth until they started to hurt.

'We don't know if he's done anything Ben. He's upset. He's crying his heart out up there.'

'What's he doing crashing in like that.'

I shouted upstairs. 'If you've left that damn bicycle on the driveway, I swear I'll run over it in the morning.' And it would be his own fault.

Abigail sighed, 'Please Ben, calm down – look you go and sit down, I'll put the kettle on.' She guided me away from the staircase and toward the table.

'Did he even remember what I sent him out for? I doubt it. I've got to finish up in the study.'

I shouted one last warning up the stairs, 'You've got five minutes or I'm coming up!' Then I stormed out of the room toward the study.

Abigail stood for a second or two, then gathered herself and went to put the kettle on. As I went into the study I heard, 'God, I need something stronger than tea!'

About an hour later there was a loud knock on the front door. It sounded urgent. Abigail went to answer it. I heard the voices from my room.

'This way officer,' then 'Elliot! Come downstairs please.'

There was a pause 'NOW!'

Officer! The police! Always be pleasant to the police! I went back into the kitchen.

'Good evening officers, how can we help you?'

The officer said 'Are you Mr Elliot Saphan, sir?'

'I'm his father. What has he done?'

THE BOOK OF MAEVE

*T*he family grew; well the two of us, three, I suppose, if you count Dot as a sort of honorary Grandma. And so did the business. Not in an empirical way, but in an Elina, Dot, and Maeve sort of way. Slowly, locally, methodically. It grew with small, but regular, orders from word of mouth recommendations, backed up with friendly service and quality goods.

I suppose I grew with it and learned to sweep up the discarded stalks and bits of wrapping, and tidy around the shop, while Elina worked happily away. My favourite job was jumping on the unwanted cardboard boxes to flatten them for the bin-men to take away every other Monday.

One day, when I was about five, Elina got me up early, 'Come on Maeve darling, it's a big day for you today.'

'What? Big day? It must be my birthday, oh hooray!'

There didn't seem to be any presents about.

'Breakfast is ready, then we must be off to school. Put on your new uniform.'

'School?' I don't go to school, I go to nursery, that's my place. She must mean that. Silly Elina. The red jumper was nice though. When we set off in the van, Elina started driving the wrong way. 'It's the other way Elina.'

'No dear,' she said, 'Today is your first day at proper school.'

I started to object. 'Wasn't nursery school "proper"? – What about my friends? – I won't know anyone, I want to be home with you.'

Elina smiled, 'Not any more, now you're starting school. You'll make lots of new friends and you'll be home afterwards.'

Afterwards, how long was afterwards? I thought that afterwards I wouldn't have to go again. How wrong was I?

I actually got on very well at school; at least the teachers and Elina seemed pleased with me and, to be honest, after that first day, I enjoyed it immensely. Elina had to close the shop early during the week though to fit in with school hours. Even though Dot was still with us, she wasn't getting any younger and Elina thought it wasn't fair to ask her to look after the shop on her own. My school reports from primary school all said the same things, 'She's a bright girl with a bright future. A little headstrong at times, but full of confidence, and that can't be a bad thing.'

It was only when I started secondary school that things started to change. I liked studying but there was an element in class who did not, and they frowned on anyone who seemed to get better grades than them. That's not quite true either, they didn't just frown, they made their feelings a lot clearer. Firstly, Jane Pedersen always wanted to be first. She was typical; she was tall, blonde, of course, and athletic – not that you would see her anywhere near a sports field voluntarily. Her brother, on the other hand, was heavily into sport and played football. In fact he played so well that he had been invited to go to the football academy and hoped to be scouted for greater things. Jane made sure everyone knew this and how important and potentially wealthy it made her and her family. She had two acolytes, almost the image of herself. They followed her everywhere and laughed at her jokes. They were 'The Clones'; they had it all and they weren't shy about letting everyone know it. And if that superiority could be accentuated by comparison to a lesser being, all the better. Therefore every opportunity to point out differences was eagerly grasped, particularly when it was at the expense of a smaller, less athletic looking, more studious, not white, not blonde person like myself.

It wasn't fair. In year six, the final year of primary education, all my friends said they were going to South Street Secondary, so I pestered Elina to let me go there too. Unfortunately, due to personal circumstances, and catchment areas, it didn't turn out that way, and I found myself largely on my own. My confidence in the order of the world around me dwindled. With no support group of friends I became an easy target for the clones whenever I was in their vicinity, which was every day.

Around that time, the rash started. It appeared across my face, mostly on my cheeks.

'It's probably just your pores getting clogged up,' Elina said, or 'It's just your age.'

I used creams and lotions on it, and only the purest, most expensive soap, and – nothing. There it remained, displayed across my face for all to see. Fortunately, being mixed race, my skin was fairly dark so it didn't stand out like a beacon, but it was noticeable. Certainly at a distance of about three metres and, during the course of a school day, at no time is anyone as far away as three metres.

I started getting tired easily, 'Come on Lucas, join in. We all get tired. Grow yourself a backbone.' This from the gym teacher. No-one believed me, they thought I was trying to get away with something. I was in and out of the chemist's quite regularly, for different things, and had been offered a variety of medicines for aches, rashes, and so on.

Then there was the unwell sort of feelings that would come and go regularly and which I, and others, attributed to the normal problems faced by every growing girl. Elina said 'It's the hormones causing spots, they'll clear up in no time.'

The rash remained, displayed across my face for all to see. It didn't go unremarked. Later I discovered that these rashes came and went, but at the time I thought it was forever. I took to lying on the bed at weekends instead of going out. The queasiness started, on a daily basis.

'I'm sure it's an allergy,' Elina had remarked, 'Everyone has allergies these days, it's the pollution.'

So a period of trial and error commenced. There were charts for everything, all categorised.

Foods:
Fresh green,
Preserved green,
Fresh meat red,
Fresh meat white,
Dry foods sweet,
Dry foods savoury.
Liquids of all kinds
And lists below each heading.

It was so hard to keep track of what had been tried, what

had been avoided and what combination hadn't, and nothing much changed anyway, so Elina finally picked up the phone.

'Hello, I need to see the doctor please – yes, an appointment. Elina Lucas – no, it's not for me – it's for my daughter, Maeve. Yes, Maeve Lucas – third of April, 2006. We are registered to this surgery, yes. We need to talk to the doctor about that. I've been researching it and it says lupus something. No – No – Yes – What? How long? three weeks? She could die in three weeks. 111 – yes I know about 111. No, she's not dying. Alright then, three weeks.'

So three weeks it was. Three more weeks of pain in my legs, feeling ill, this ugly rash, and a plethora of new symptoms coming and going. I thought I was becoming a hypochondriac and, sadly, so did the school. However, three weeks came and went and we turned up at the surgery in plenty of time. Sod's law states that if you are on time, then the appointments will be running late; if you are late, then there will have been some cancellations and you will therefore miss your appointment. We were early, so we had a lengthy wait. Despite the receptionist's occasional cheery 'Don't worry, won't be long now,' we sat there and watched as a variety of patients came and went.

Elina said 'I got the earliest I could – so they wouldn't have time to get behind, and it's with Dr. Mambwe, so keep your eyes on the screen there.'

'Is he new?' I asked. My head was splitting apart.

'I don't know, and it's she. Dr Mambwe is a she.'

'Will she take long?'

'I don't know darling, but she will have all your notes. She's probably reading them now.'

As if by magic Maeve's name showed on the screen and the

loudspeaker said, 'Maeve Lucas, Dr Mambwe, room three please,' as impersonally as it could. There. *Finally!*

Elina helped me through to the doctor's room as my legs were feeling quite painful. When I say *quite*, I mean it as a relative term, compared to how bad they have felt recently.

Room number three had a smiley sign on it saying '3'

Elina knocked on the door, polite as always. A voice said 'Come!'

She opened the door and ushered me in first. 'Hello Doctor, thank you for seeing us,' she said.

'Come in. Sit down please,' said the doctor; a small, pinched, African looking woman. She didn't even look at us, but at the screen on her desk.

'I see from your phone call, that you think you have lupus? What do you think I can do for you today?'

I started, 'I just feel awful – ' but Elina cut in.

'I've looked up all the symptoms and, as I said to the woman when I called, it said lupus thingy.'

Dr. Mambwe said, without turning round, 'There is nothing in the notes to ring any alarm bells. Mrs Lucas, do you or your husband have any issues that may be hereditary?'

Elina was surprised, 'No, nothing like this at all. I am divorced now, but my husband was a healthy man.'

'Mmm,' was the doctor's reply.

And then, as an afterthought Elina added 'Although I do remember he did have a sort of epilepsy, I think is the closest I can come – but Maeve is adopted. I can't answer for her birth parents.'

The doctor typed something on the keyboard in front of her, but said nothing. Elina leaned in toward her, almost conspiratorially, 'She's not sleeping and getting terrible joint pains, so she has trouble walking, and she's feeling sick all of the time.'

The doctor continued, 'You've been taking Aceta-minophen for a while – '

'On and off – ' Elina cut in.

'and Nystaform for the rashes,' as if she hadn't noticed the interruption. 'Have you seen a rheumatologist? There's nothing here about any recent visits.'

Elina told her, 'No – nobody's mentioned rheumatologists. Do we need to make an appointment?'

Still not looking at us, the doctor seemed to be reading notes from the screen on her desk. 'I think this is probably all about anxiety which could be caused by anything. Stress? Have there been any problems? Are you worried about anything in particular?'

I said, 'Only about feeling like this.'

'What about at school, any exams coming up?'

There weren't any. 'No.'

I don't know if she heard but she carried on anyway, 'It could be diet. What about allergies? Have you been tested?'

'We've spent weeks going through all of that, and we're very careful,' Elina said.

Finally the doctor turned to me. 'You must address these personal issues. There is very little I can do except perhaps give you some benzodiazepine for anxiety.'

'Benzo – dia – ?' Elina stopped.

'It's Valium,' Dr Mambwe said, a little condescendingly I thought. 'Are you taking hydroxychloroquine? There's no mention of it here.'

She was now looking at me but Elina answered 'No, what's that?'

'They may have said Plaquenil. It helps with swelling and pain in the joints. Really, a rheumatologist is the person you should see. I'll make a note. In the meantime – I'll give you a letter to go and see the nurse to get some current blood samples from you and we'll see how it is all behaving.' She turned back to the screen.

Elina was confused. 'Is that it? Is that all you can do? Just some more tablets. To what? Help her relax?' The doctor ignored her and wrote a prescription.

'Lupus is an incurable condition. It's an auto immune disease, which means that from time to time the body attacks itself. At different times there are different issues and if you do have it, which I doubt really, all I, or anyone, can do is treat the symptoms that we're presented with. I'm sorry. Now, I do have others to see. Good day.'

She wrote a letter of referral and handed it, with the prescription, to Elina. She was dismissing us.

'I am sorry, there is nothing more I can do. It's something you're going to have to manage.'

We felt we were being rushed out of the office so the doctor could make her daily target. We hadn't been in there for ten minutes.

Elina drove us home, stopping at the chemist's to get the tablets. As soon as we got home, I had to go to bed. Elina, meanwhile, went onto the computer and the internet was consulted once again. It didn't agree. It screamed *Lupus!*

We found a rheumatologist, it seemed as if they all have very long waiting lists, and we secured an appointment. Fortune tried to smile weakly upon us as Elina had managed to bully them into giving us a cancellation appointment. Following that, arguments and further consultations followed. A second rheumatologist was approached, and finally a sort of diagnosis was reached.

'Maeve, we have the results of your tests, but I'm afraid they're inconclusive' he said, 'You *may* have Lupus.'

To give it its full and proper name, because it makes a full and proper mess, it is Systemic Lupus Erythematosus. After that, there were the seemingly interminable tests: blood tests, ANA tests, tests for Raynaud's phenomenon, pulmonary hypertension, and on and on.

This affected me in many ways. Apart from the regular tests, I had to be careful about everything I ate or drank. Although I wasn't strictly allergic to certain foods, they would still have an adverse effect. Though I tended toward vegetarianism anyway, I was only safe from flare ups on the condition that I stuck to organic foods. Water was another problem, or the fluoride present in tap water was. I could only drink water from a known source, i.e. bottled water with a guaranteed provenance. That didn't help my situation at school, because now I also had to be careful of food cooked in water containing fluoride. School meals were out, so gone was that opportunity to mix with other students. I occasionally suffered from seizures, which marked me out as 'weak'. Sometimes I had to be taken out of class to lie down due to fatigue and pain in my legs. Some days I felt so bad I couldn't go to school at all. When I did, however, and the rash appeared, the clones saw it as a challenge to make sure as many people as possible knew about it and the gruesome consequences of being anywhere in my vicinity. According to them, to merely think about associating with me risked catching and developing this galloping nameless condition into a life threatening 'lurgy'. Unfortunately, and unbeknownst to me, or them, at the time, that's exactly what it was. There was, is, nothing contagious about it though. Apparently you have it, or you don't. It's a condition not a disease. It only appears once one has started to develop, and then mainly to women; one of which I had recently become. All this was also noted by the clones, and they were well practised in weaponising the flaws of the weak.

Bless her, Elina tried everything she could think of. She started taking me to the church for 'healing' – that's where I first met Elliot – and she would subject me to any homespun recipe that she heard about from friends, customers, or even waiting in line at the chemist. Even though there were various medicines to control the symptoms, and we had them all, they weren't perfect and didn't always have the desired effect.

I sort of retreated into my shell, like the proverbial turtle on sensing trouble. I became rather shy of people. I rarely went out, and refused any invitation that involved a gathering of more than just the closest friends. Closest friends, in actual fact, meant Elina and Dot .

There was Elliot, of course.

Elliot was older by about three or four years. We'd met, or got to know each other, at the church. He was always at the church services, particularly the healing services, with his father, Ben Saphan: Pastor. The name was unmissable on the notice board outside.

He seemed very shy at first, but when we got to know each other a little better he told me about the church fire years ago, when his mother and baby sister had died. The church itself hadn't burned, that was the pastor's house, and apparently it was only through the pastor's bravery and selflessness that Elliot had survived; even though he had been injured quite badly.

These days the smell of green was everywhere. It surrounded me. It was comforting. It smelled good. It had been the backdrop to every day of the sixteen and a bit years of my life. It came up the rickety stairs leading from the flower shop, and laid itself against each surface as a sort of olfactory veneer. It was the green of cut grasses, leaves, and crushed stems. I knew them all. The only smell that I could recall that wasn't permeated forever green was my father. He wasn't my real father though, as Mum – Elina as I called her – had told me. I had been adopted, or 'chosen', when I was a baby. He had been a big man, probably still was. As a three year old – which is probably as far back as I can remember – of course any man would appear big, but he seemed to have been big in every way. His laugh had filled the whole space. He didn't block out the sun, he intensified its warmth and when he hugged, his shiny suit became the world. He left so long ago that I could hardly remember anything about him, except the lovely sandalwood aftershave smell that always seemed to surround him. And the feeling that I was safe whenever he held me, even if the whole world collapsed. Which was ironic really, because when it did, he wasn't there.

'Hola, Alexa,' called Elina's voice from the living room, 'Enciende la radio! Sintonice radio dos.' Steve Wright's voice filled the room. 'Hola Alexa! Bajale el volumen!' I could hear the kettle beginning its climax as the volume of Steve Wright's Love Songs decreased. 'Maeve! Are you ready? Kettle's on.'

At the sound of her voice, little Rosie, our Coton de Tuléar friend, bounded off the foot of the bed – where she had her safe place – through my legs, out of the small room and into the kitchen in a flash of white fluff. Food was in the air.

'Coming Elina, just brushing my hair. Or what's left of it!' I shouted.

Green represents growth and rebirth, not death and decay; which was how I felt every morning nowadays. I had everything that I wanted. No, strike that, I had everything that I needed. What I wanted was good health, and I didn't have that. I used to have, up until a couple of years ago when it all started to go wrong.

'How long does it take to brush your hair?' Elina called.

'Less and less each day, apparently.' I bundled what there was of my hair on top of my head and tied it there, hoping that if it was tied properly, then people wouldn't see the patches; which probably weren't actually as visible to others as they were to me but, nonetheless, they were there. I looked in the small, wood framed mirror, plucking the hairbrush clean. *It will not win. Today will be a good day!* The smile the mirror returned to me wasn't at all convincing. I strode the two paces across the bedroom and out into the living room.

'Which kind would you like this morning love?' called Elina from the kitchen, 'Ginger, Green, Echinacea, decaffeinated Lapsang Souchong? – All right Rosie darling, it's coming.' She opened the tin of dog food and emptied half into Rosie's bowl, having to hold her back with one hand while she did so.

'Fun-ny,' I replied, 'Just a fruit juice, please.'

Out of the window, in the street below, there were people out and about, and some traffic; but it was Sunday so not as many as usual. I wonder how their day started.

'Here you are, what do you want for breakfast?'

'Just a scrambled egg, if that's okay. I'm not that hungry.'

'Coming right up! Make sure you're ready though, there's not a lot of wiggle room this morning,' said Elina.

'Is it all ready, or do you need me to do anything?' I asked.

'No, it's all done,' said Elina, 'Dot and I sorted it last night. It just needs loading. Bread or toast?'

'Toast please.'

'I'll have to make another loaf when we get back, we're quite low.'

The Carpenters were singing about birds suddenly appearing. Elina made a funny noise, like a warm hum, and started moving to the music. 'This was our song, back in the day,' she murmured, 'Hola Alexa, sube la radio.'

Elina had been given an Amazon Echo for her birthday, Dot had been as helpful as always, but electronics seemed to be a little beyond her capacity, one might say. They had unpacked it together and as they set it on the dresser they heard the shop bell give its cheery tinkle, 'You get it dear,' said Dot. 'My knees and those stairs aren't the best of friends.' Elina hesitated, 'Go! It's only small, it can't be that hard.' Elina had gone. The customer was taking his time choosing whatever it was he might have wanted, leaving Dot to decipher the *setting up* pictures in the instructions. Dot's eyesight, bless her, wasn't getting any better as she got older, and the instructions were a little confusing. The result was that she set it up successfully, paired it with the radio, but got the wrong language setting and now it would only respond to Spanish. Neither of them could figure out how to change it back. Now, they were used to it and decided to stop fretting and to leave it as it was.

'Hola Alexa, sube la radio un poco mas.' It was an oldie then, but a great song is a great song. It was odd that she had been thinking of him too.

The smell of eggs and toast cooking overlaid the green, and I fetched cutlery from the drawer. Elina put the eggs and toast on a plate and, dancing around Rosie, who was pushing her bowl around the kitchen with her nose, put it on the table.

'Is that what you listened to Elina?' I asked, speaking as I started on the eggs. I was hungrier than I thought. 'Back then?'

'Then and now. I loved to dance to this, especially with your dad. He would sing it to me as we moved.'

'Why aren't there any pictures of you both around?'

'Oh, we couldn't afford pictures.' Elina stopped. 'It wasn't like now, when everyone photographs their breakfast you know. When you took a picture, you had to wait until the roll of film was finished, then take it to the chemist, leave it there for a week, then go back and collect it, pay for it of course. All without knowing whether the pictures were any good or not.'

'What do you mean, any good?'

'Sometimes they were very out of focus and blurry, or the camera had moved, or something, so they didn't get developed. You still had to pay for them though.'

'Someone else got to see all your photos before you did?'

'Yes, I suppose so.'

'And they chose which ones you got?'

'I know. It sounds odd nowadays, with the unlimited digital and all. At that time you only got a roll of film with – I think it was twenty four, or maybe thirty six – on it. I don't remember exactly.'

'What was the point of that – if you couldn't see the photos 'til weeks after you took them?'

'But that's the way it was.'

'So you couldn't post them then?'

'Yes, in an envelope.'

'What?' This was getting confusing. 'I meant on Insta.'

'Oh, Maeve, there was nothing like that. If you wanted to send them to anyone, you had to send them in the post. You know that digital only really got popular just after you were born. That's just how it was, and everyone accepted it.'

'Really?'

'Yes,' she said, checking her watch. 'Now come along, I'll see if I can find some old photos later if you really want, but we have to get moving. I'll take Rosie out for a minute, and hope she goes, then we must be off.'

'Is it hereditary?' I asked, pointing to the rash on my face.

'I wouldn't know, love. You'd have to look that one up,' she replied as she attached Rosie's lead and tugged her to the stairs.

'Hola Alexa, baja la radio,' I said.

I didn't, couldn't, finish the toast, but drained the fruit juice while Elina took Rosie downstairs. I took the plate into the kitchen and sluiced it under the tap, rinsed out the cup, found the van keys, and followed them. The van was parked in the alley behind the shop, close to the wall to leave just enough room for another vehicle to get past. Unless it was Sunday night, when it was parked out front because the dustbin lorry came early on a Monday morning and wouldn't otherwise be able to make it along the alleyway to empty the other shops' bins. That had been the cause of heated debate on various occasions in the past. The rear door of the shop was open, as Elina had just taken Rosie that way. There was a small patch of grass about fifty yards or so along the alley that Rosie liked to use, and I could see Elina standing there encouraging the little dog. I unlocked the white Ford Courier van and opened the back doors.

Elina shouted, 'They're on the table, all marked "Saphan".' So

I returned inside and started picking up the bundles of flowers and loading them in.

'Thanks Lovey,' said Elina, on her way back through the shop with Rosie; who had been very obliging and completed her business in record time. 'Take it easy now, I'll be with you in a second.'

I was beginning to feel tired already. These days I was always feeling tired, and my legs ached like mad. 'Do we have to go Elina?' I called.

'They're not going to deliver themselves, are they baby?'

'No, I mean do we both have to go? I'm really tired.'

'Yes, and you know why. Just sit in the front, I'll finish load-ing. It won't take a minute.'

'I'll look it up when we get back. You don't mind me saying, do you?'

'What? – Oh the rash thing. No. Look Maeve, we always said, and it's still true, even though he's not here anymore, we always said if you wanted to find out. It's okay. It's part of your journey, as it were.'

I squeezed the passenger door open and manoeuvred myself into the seat while Elina loaded in the remaining flowers. She locked up the shop. 'Rosie's quite happily back on your bed, and I've left the radio on for her. Cheer up, it might never happen.'

'It already did, remember.'

She looked at me, not quite in the eye. There was no answer to that. When we got to the church, Elliot would be there; he always seemed to be around, somewhere, looking. He was an odd fish. I liked him though. He wasn't pushy or grabby like the other boys.

It wasn't a long drive and the roads were clear, so it only took a few minutes to get there. There was only one other car in the car park so far, and that was the pastor's. Everybody knew that car, a big black Wolseley with running boards, like the gangster ones in the films. Elina parked the van as near to the main doors as she could, leapt out and opened the rear. As she did so, the pastor appeared, looking at his watch.

'Cutting it a little fine aren't we?'

'Morning, Mr Saphan,' she called out cheerily, ignoring his comment. 'One or two issues to deal with, but there are the two of us, we'll soon have it looking it's best, just in time for the service.'

Before I had even lifted my thoughts away from my own ills and come back to the present, Elina was already unloading the flowers. The pastor took a step back to allow Elina passage into the church, 'Will you be joining us in the healing again today, Maeve?'

'Well,' I said, 'I'm not at my best.'

'Perfect timing,' he continued, 'The Lord works in mysterious ways.'

'Come along Maeve, you collect the old ones and I'll do the arranging – chop chop.' encouraged Elina.

I scrambled along behind as best I could.

'And don't forget to bring the big bag,' Elina called over her shoulder.

'Sorry!' I changed direction suddenly and hurried back to get the bin bag sized container. It wasn't exactly a bag, it was stiffer than that, but it wasn't a box either; it was softer. It wasn't heavy however, and it was used to collect the flowers that had been there from the previous week; but not to crush them, as they were to be sorted through and delivered to the old peoples' homes in the town. As I took it inside, I glanced around, subconsciously perhaps, to see if Elliot was around. I hadn't known him long, but we did seem to have some sort of a connection. He wasn't there anyway.

The instant I started collecting the flowers, the energy just drained out of my entire body. 'I've got to sit down,' I said, 'Sorry, did I say that aloud? I've just gone really tired.'

'Do you need a drink of water?' Pastor Saphan was at the altar and had noticed. I tried to be strong, I was supposed to be a help not a hindrance.

'No, I'll be fine, just need a minute.'

Elina was concerned. A minute wasn't going to help. 'Go and sit in the van, love. I'll take you home as soon as we've done.'

The pastor again, 'Just stay here and rest. If you like, there is a sofa in the vestry you could lay down on.'

'Would that be too much trouble? I mean we don't want to impose, and isn't it sort of private back there?' I said.

'Don't worry about any of that, it's just a room.'

Elina continued 'Won't the service be starting soon? I mean, we've almost finished?'

'That's alright, Maeve can rest in there,' the pastor replied, then to me, 'You can close your eyes for a bit if you like.'

'I really don't feel so good.'

The pastor carried on, 'The service lasts about an hour, as you already know, so we should be finished by, oh, usually 12.15 or so. Look if you're up to it, we have the healing service following Sunday worship. When you're rested, you can take part in that.' Elina had started to bring me to these 'healings' once a month.

'I do need to lie down Elina.' I felt so heavy, I could hardly lift my legs.

'If you're sure then, Pastor?'

'Ben.'

'Ben,' Elina repeated. Between them they settled me down comfortably on the sofa, gave me a glass of water, from a bottle of course, closed the door, and went back into the body of the church.

'You carry on, she'll be perfectly alright there. The service starts soon. Plenty of time to do whatever it is you're going to do. By the time you're back I'm sure she'll be right as rain.'

Elina had tried every known remedy – and even some unknown ones – that she thought might help alleviate the different symptoms that kept revealing themselves, and then disappearing; rather like an evil game of hide and seek. She had heard that, back in the day, there had been some quite miraculous cures attributed to the church and that particular pastor. Some even said that it was by direct intervention of God through him that Elliot had survived the awful fire but there hadn't been any such 'miracles' since that time. However, people, like Prometheus, live in hope and the church still attracted a fair number of the faithful, believing that one day, maybe even this day, there may be another. It was an avenue that Elina couldn't leave untried, so she had been attending the services regularly, most particularly those that included a 'healing' at the end of them; she'd make me take my place among the supplicants. The added benefit of this was that Elina got to know the pastor and arranged a regular supply of flowers for the services, and recommendations for the weddings and funerals that took place there.

I had been to so many of these healing services that I had got to know some of the helpers by name, Elliot among them, but I had not been healed. *How could I? Lupus is incurable.* The body attacks itself because it mistakes good cells for bad cells; there's only symptoms to treat. Nevertheless Elina made me go. 'Miracles are just that! Miracles! They don't have any sense or logic and they can happen to anyone at any time!'

During the services the pastor even warns all those present, that 'The Lord God himself is omnipotent and almighty and He alone has the power to heal. He will choose, in His infinite wisdom, those who will be physically healed and those who will be healed in the spirit, for without giving ourselves to Him, and repenting of our sins, there can be no healing.'

So, obviously it was my fault. It was my lack of commitment, faith, and repentance that was blocking my miracle.

This Sunday followed the pattern of all the others. I could hear it all from the vestry. Everyone started arriving at the specified time and I assume sat in the usual seats, nodding to all the 'season ticket holders' around them. To help set the mood for the oncoming battle with the forces of evil, the heavenly choir sung muted choruses of well known hymns, only just audible above the low hum of the congregation. At the appropriate time, and as with any self respecting theatrical performance, the lights dimmed slightly, the volume of the choir increased, and the audi – sorry, the congregation fell silent. Then suddenly, lights flashed brighter, the choir became joyous, and Ben Saphan, pastor, vicar of God, took centre stage.

'Hallelujah!' he shouted.

'Hallelujah!' everyone replied.

'Brothers and Sisters, we are gathered together here today in the name of the Lord Jesus Christ, and he promises us. Promises. Us! That whenever two or more people are gathered together in His name. He will be there. Are there two believers here today?'

The congregation, almost as one, replied 'Yes!'

'Then the Lord Himself is among us. Turn to your brother or sister beside you, take their hand, and tell them that the Lord is among us today.'

There was a general low level of people's voices repeating his words, punctuated by the odd 'Amen,' and 'Praise His name.'

'We will now join together and sing to His glory, accompanied by our very own celestial choir!'

The choir stood up resplendent in their blue and gold coloured robes, and started to sing; the congregation arose slightly slower and started late but caught up quickly. After the hymn, and before anyone had time to get comfortable again, Ben was on his feet.

'Is anyone among you in trouble?'

Congregation, 'Yes, we are.'

'Let them pray.' He continued, 'Is anyone happy? Let them sing songs of praise.'

Congregation again, 'We will sing to the Lord.'

'Is anyone among you sick? Let them call the elders of the church to pray over them and anoint them in the name of the Lord. And the prayer offered in faith will make the sick person well; the Lord will raise them up. If they have sinned, they will be forgiven.'

Congregation once more, 'Amen!'

'Therefore confess your sins to each other and pray for each other so that you may be healed. The prayer of a righteous person is powerful and effective.'

'Amen!' chorused all.

Then there were prayers, another hymn, and the sermon; which that day was based on Ecclesiastes 1:14. Ben Saphan expounded the futility of pursuing worldly things as being like 'chasing the wind' for a full twenty minutes, then another hymn; the sudden introduction of which startled everyone from their stupor. Following that hymn was the 'healing'.

Ben Saphan took centre stage, one of his helpers brought a white robe out and put it on him, then he symbolically washed his hands.

'Praise the Lord,' he called out.

'Amen!' from the congregation

'How good it is to sing praises to our God,

how pleasant and fitting to praise him!

The Lord builds up Jerusalem;

he gathers the exiles of Israel.

He heals the broken-hearted

and binds up their wounds.

All those who wish to call upon the Lord and be healed, come forward.'

There was a general shuffling. While the helpers, including Elliot, went out into the congregation to help those who wanted to, to come forward, helping with walking aids, pushing a wheelchair, or simply guiding them forward, Ben signalled across the congregation to where he had spotted Elina return-ing. She got up and made her way along the side of the pews to the little door to the vestry. It was already open so she slipped quietly through.

I wasn't asleep, but lying down for an hour had helped. I had been listening to the service, the calling out and singing, and the energy in the place. Elina helped me up, and fussed about tidying me up, then we went quietly, past the door to the helpers dressing room, and back into the body of the church. Ben helped me up onto the stage and Elina sat down in an empty space on a pew near the front. Elliot had come out of the little door and had gone to the back of the stage to set down a small table with a decanter and a couple of glasses, then took his place with the others and waited to be called. Ben summoned one of the other helpers to come and look after me.

When everyone who wanted to, or who could fit onto the stage area, had come forward, Ben went to the helpers, one by one, said something quietly to each and then turned to the front again "In Psalm 107, oh Lord, you promise that when we call out to you, the eternal one, you will heal and rescue us from certain death. We believe there is no illness you cannot heal, as the bible tells us that you can raise people even from the dead. We ask for your healing here today. We also know, Almighty God, that not all are healed, but our hearts remain soft to you that we may understand your plan." Ben turned to the first supplicant

'Oh God we thank you that – ' he whispered to the helper standing in close attendance, 'What is the given name?'

The helper asked the man's name.

'John,' he said. The helper then repeated this to the pastor.

'John. What is your affliction from which you seek the help of the Lord?'

John looked a little nonplussed at the formality of the question, but held his nerve. 'My knee doesn't work properly,' he said.

Ben then stood really close to John, almost touching noses, and then loudly enough for John to take a step back, Ben cried out.

'We thank you that our brother John belongs to you, but he is suffering with his knee. Oh Lord we ask that you show your infinite mercy and lift his burden from him, in the name of Jesus. Amen.'

Then he grabbed John's knee, causing a gasp of pain to

escape from him and forcing him backwards into the arms of the helper behind him, who held him tightly in what looked to all concerned like a bear hug. At this point the congregation erupted into a gasp, then an audible letting out of their breath, followed by an 'Amen!' and John was escorted to a seat at the side to recover.

Ben Saphan then turns to the next supplicant: me.

'Hello Maeve,' he said, 'we are all praying for you today.'

I said a simple 'Thank you.' – *what else could I say?* – and waited.

'Oh God we thank you that our sister Maeve belongs to you, afflicted with this foul condition and we ask once again that you show your infinite mercy and lift her burden from her, in the name of Jesus. Amen.'

I was just thinking calling it a foul condition in public like this wasn't going to do me any favours, when Ben Saphan slapped my forehead, harder than I thought was strictly necessary, and pushed me back against the helper standing behind. I was then held and hugged by the helper, and escorted away.

Again the church erupted. 'Amen!'

The next in line was a large, quite nervous, woman who kept glancing toward the doors of the church, and moistening her lips. Ben nodded at Elliot as the next helper and he came and stood behind her. Ben reached over to the little table behind him, poured a small amount of coloured water into one of the glasses, and offered it to the woman.

'Now, remember your promise? Don't be nervous, God is with us to give us strength.'

'Th-th-thank you,' she said and drank it in one go. Ben handed the glass to another helper and continued,

'Oh God, we thank you that – '

Elliot asked her what her name was, 'L-L-Lucy, Lucy Greal-ley' she stammered 'I r-r-really – '

'Yes, I know Lucy,' said Ben, carrying on regardless. 'Oh God we thank you that – '

'And I h-h-have an infection – er – in my water – we spoke – ' she continued, 'and I n-n-need to – '

Too late, Ben was already in full stride 'Our sister Lucy belongs to you, she is suffering with an infection and we ask that you show your infinite mercy and lift her burden from her, in the name of Jesus. Amen.'

Ben then placed his hand just below Lucy's stomach and pushed her into Elliot, She let out what could only be called a high pitched squeak as she fell, Elliot caught her and helped her to straighten up. He steadied her so she didn't fall backwards, though she wasn't small, he hugged her and led her to one side.

Again 'Amen!' filled the church.

The healing continued until the supplicants had been blessed in turn. There were final calls of 'Glory be!' and 'Praise the Lord!', before the choir stood up again and started to sing *He Calleth Thee*, the hymn that Ben liked to signify the end of the service. As it was coming to a close he again took centre stage and cried 'God be with you as you make your way this week, my brothers and sisters, and may the Lord walk with you as you face your own trials, great and small. We are here as always, in His name, to help and assist you, so don't be shy about dropping in to see us at our regular sessions up at the Wellness Centre, also private healing by appointment, as you know, and as some of you can attest to the benefits through the Grace of God.'

'Please stand for the benediction'

He raised his arms aloft.

'And the very God of peace sanctify you wholly. And I pray God your whole spirit and soul and body be preserved blameless unto the coming of our Lord Jesus Christ. Amen.'

This was followed by another general chorus of 'Amen!' and Ben slumped into a chair at the back of the stage. A helper brought him a glass of water, and another went off for a mop to clean up a small puddle on the stage.

When the service finished I went back to sit with Elina and waited with her. She wanted to pass on a note of thanks that she had been given, for the flowers, to the pastor. He had recovered in time to be at the main door saying goodbye to the congregation, spending a little more time with those that had come to be healed and giving them invitations to join him at the reiki clinic in town; for a small discount of course. When most people had left and he was free, Elina went to see him and I wandered outside. Cars were leaving the car park, people were walking out in small groups. The large woman who was at the healing was having difficulty getting into a small car, she seemed to be crying and eating at the same time. Nobody seemed to take much notice of her. I thought the philosophy of the church, generally speaking, was to help people. No-one was helping her. It must be quite selective then.

The buzz of conversation could still be heard, but it was fading into the distance. Suddenly Elliot was beside me. Elliot was older by about three or four years. I'd first come across him at the church, when I came forward with the other hopeful souls. I'd seen him in the background, putting out or collecting hymn books, and generally helping out. Apparently he had suffered terrible burns to his hands and had had to wear gloves all the time because the scarring had been so severe. I wasn't sure how true that all was because his hands looked perfectly okay to me, but the pastor did refer to it regularly. In fact he made quite a big thing of Elliot and how, suddenly, after a healing service, miraculously, the scars had gone. Word spread like wildfire after that and congregation numbers had increased so much that, for a while, it was hard to get a seat. I think that's when Elina first heard of the services.

Elliot is always there, where people can see him, during the healings. On show. Holding people that the pastor has treated and escorting them back to their seats. From his expression he doesn't seem to like the drama and emotion that goes with it all. I think it may be all a little over dramatic, the way people collapse or cry out, perhaps because they believe that they should, or maybe they really are caught up in the emotion of it all. I've heard that religious trances can do that sort of thing, in other countries, other cultures, but not here, surely. Rarely, if ever, do I see anyone throw walking sticks away and dance back down the aisle. But Elliot's hands are undeniable.

Anyway I often saw him around the place on his bike. We became sort of distant friends, though not having any actual connecting opportunities apart from the church services, and waving, or nodding, to each other when we passed. This grew to an exchange of pleasantries at the church, and an exchange of numbers. Occasionally he might bump into me, accidentally on purpose, on the way out of the grounds. If that happened – and it did, most particularly if Elina had to wait to discuss some flower arrangements with the pastor – then Elliot would smile, and stand awkwardly trying to think of something to talk about other than 'I saw you at the healing?' or, the lame 'Do you come here often?'

Because he knew I did. So, 'Hi.' was about it.

So it wasn't altogether unexpected or strange that he should stop and talk now. I was waiting by the flower van in the car park, and Elliot pushed his bike casually over,

'Hi!' he said, unsurprisingly. 'I saw you in the church.'

I looked at him. *Was he serious?* 'Yes, I know. I was standing right by you.'

'Course, but before that, you were in the vestry. What were you doing there?'

'I wasn't feeling well, so the pastor let me rest in there for a bit.' I told him.

'Are you okay now?' Elliot asked

'Better thanks, I'll be alright when I get back home. How did you see me, the door was closed?'

'No you must have left it open – at least it was when I came past.' I noticed a bandage on his wrist and I was about to say something when he continued, 'Those healing services don't work you know. I know they say they did once, back in the day. But they don't.'

'A lot of people believe they do, and they worked for you according to the pastor.' I don't know why I was defending them, 'It gives them hope.'

'I suppose. It wasn't the service though. It's – I'm learning reiki, at the wellness centre. That can really help. It cures all sorts,' he said.

'Yeah, right,' I told him, a little sarcastically. 'I'll give it a try, when I win the lottery!'

Elina had mentioned the reiki centre, or the Hannah Saphan Centre for Wellness as it was officially called. To me, it sounded like one of those alternative treatments that hippies made up.

Elliot persisted though. 'I know it costs a lot, but it is based on Japanese principles of medicine going back hundreds of years.'

'But, how can it work – it's ridiculous.' Well, it was.

All Elliot said was 'You'd be surprised.' Then he added, 'Look, I'll text you, see how you're doing. Perhaps we can meet up? I'm finished inside,' he pointed to the church, 'the church.'

'I've got a fair bit to do today, I won't be free.'

'You work at that flower shop.' Not a question more of a statement.

'Yes, Lucas's Lupins'

'So, it's your van. Nice.'

'No, it's Elina's. My mum's. I don't drive yet. Not for about a year or so anyhow.'

'No, no, of course. Sorry I didn't mean did you drive it, just that you sort of belonged to it,' he stammered.

'It's actually the flower shop's van.' I laughed 'And I belong to that.'

'Yes, of course. I like flowers.' I looked at him, he looked down and repeated 'I like flowers.'

'I think everyone likes flowers,' I helped, 'at least enough to keep the shop going.'

'Yeah, I'spose!'

'Elina does the flowers for the church every week.'

Encouraged, he continued, 'Oh, I wondered how they sort of appeared on a Sunday. Do you bring them yourself?'

'No, I don't drive. It needs the van.'

Embarrassed, he mumbled, 'Oh yeah, you said,' and then, seemingly overcome by his own awkwardness, 'Anyway, must dash, bye!'

As he jumped onto his bike, his foot slipped from on the pedal and consequently he missed the saddle and landed, neither foot on the ground, but sitting painfully on the cross-bar. He scrambled back to standing, looked back with a weak smile – I restrained myself from laughing out loud – and he, rather more sedately than he'd probably planned, pedalled away. I watched him go, smiling to myself. He was nice. Odd, but nice. Just then Elina came out of the church. She'd been talking to the pastor about – who knows what? – probably flowers, but she had caused a bit of a log jam inside, she said, so cut it short. We got back into the van and went home.

Before I'd even got to the top of the stairs, a little bundle of fluffy energy hit me full on; I picked her up, trying to see where I was going through the flurry of doggy kisses, 'Hello Rosie, you gorgeous little thing, have you been a good girl?' I put her down at the top of the stairs and she continued to run in circles round our feet as we entered the living room.

'Are you ready for something to eat?' This was Elina to me. I knew Rosie was ready, she was always ready.

'Yes please.'

Meals took longer than one would think in our home. We couldn't just have anything frozen out of the fridge or a take away; we had to make, I mean Elina had to make, everything from scratch. We had to know the provenance of each and every ingredient. So a sandwich, a simple sandwich, took a while. She made the bread, usually two or three loaves at a time. She froze those. Butter was out, we had substituted that with olive oil spread from a known source, and whatever I wanted inside, which was usually some vegetable concoction prepared earlier, or ugh! Oily fish. How I would love to have a white bread cheddar cheese and pickle sandwich, but that would come at a cost. Normally, huh! Nothing normal here, normally a flare up of joint inflammation, or the rash, perhaps a bout of sickness for good measure. Today, was plain roast chicken, with no gravy and some carrots and peas which Elina went to prepare.

'It'll be about an hour love!' she called from the small kitchen.

I sat down on the sofa 'Hola Alexa, enciende la radio.' I flicked through some stations, but there was nothing there that caught my interest.

'Have you got any homework to finish?' came from the kitchen.

'I'll have a look,' I said and went to get my phone. These days everything from school is on the computer, iPad or mobile. I say school, but I'm in sixth form college actually; though there is always homework so I switched it on and scrolled through.

'Hola Alexa, apagar la radio.' The Radio went off.

There were no notifications, just a text from Elliot. Surprise surprise.

Gud 2 C U after Church

I couldn't be bothered to reply. I was tired and now bored. I thought a lie down before lunch would help.

Elina called out 'Why don't you look in that drawer for those photographs I told you about.' I'd forgotten. Well, it was something to do for a minute or two.'

'Which drawer?' I asked.

'The middle one in my dresser.'

That meant in her bedroom. I went to investigate. It was a bit of a mess, I mean there were some old photos of course, and some were in those odd envelopes with a bit of film tucked in a little pocket, but there were also lots of loose ones of all shapes and sizes. I pulled them all out and took them through to the sofa where I spread them all out. In the back of the drawer with the photos was what I supposed was an old camera, just a small oblong silver box really, and a brown envelope full of baby pictures. I added it all to the pile, thinking I'd ask Elina about it, out of curiosity. There was an odd assortment. There were pictures of a little Malayan girl, I presumed that was Elina, doing lots of smiley poses in various places, including in a pineapple field. I mean who knew pineapples grew in a field?

There were pictures of lots of people and places I didn't know. It was interesting to see them, and to see Elina with her parents, but the rest meant little to me. I kept those ones out and piled the rest up. Half an hour or so to lunch, so I went to lie down. The next thing I knew was Elina standing over me with a tray, gently calling my name.

'Maeve, Maeve darling? I brought it in here for you. To save you getting up. I'll put it on the side here for you.' She placed the tray on the bedside table, and removed a reluctant Rosie.

'Oh, I found those pictures, was that you as a little girl?' I asked.

'Are they there, it's been so long. Yes, that would have been me. We went on holiday sometimes, back to where Nenek and Datuk used to live.'

'There are a lot of pictures that I don't know anyone in.'

'You finish your chicken, and I'll look at them with you. I haven't looked through those for a long time.'

'And there's a camera there. It was at the back of the drawer.'

'Was there?' Elina was surprised, 'I don't remember that. I'll have a look.'

Elina went into the living room and returned with the camera. 'Is this what you meant?'

'Yes,' I told her. 'It is a camera, isn't it?'

'It's a disposable one. You used to be able to buy them everywhere. I don't know if you still can.'

'Disposable? What you just take pictures then throw it away? How does that work?'

Elina laughed, 'No, not throw away. You returned it to the shop where you got it, or I suppose you could have even posted it, and they processed the pictures for you.'

It still sounded odd to me. 'Then what happened to the camera?'

'When you buy them, the cost of processing is included, so you don't get it back, you just buy another one.'

'So, that one hasn't been processed then?' I pressed on.

'No. I don't even know if it's been used.'

She examined the camera in her hand. 'Why, yes it has. I wonder what's on it. It's odd that it's been in the drawer. I don't remember it.'

'Ooh, a mystery. I love a mystery. Let's send it off.'

'There's still film left in it unexposed,' she told me.

'What?'

'There are still photos in it to take.'

'I'll take some of Rosie, then we can send it and get the pictures from it.'

'I don't even know if the company exists any more. I'll see if I can find out.'

I wondered, 'Can't the photo shop do it?'

'I suppose they could. They'd probably charge for it. I can't do anything today though, but it's an idea. Now eat up before it get's cold. Rosie's looking hungry.'

While Elina went back to the kitchen to tidy up, I took pictures of Rosie and nibbled at the chicken. I knew it was coming. I hadn't been feeling well all day and I wasn't really hungry. These are the signs of a flare. It's not the same for everyone; for me it's the tiredness, followed by my legs aching like mad, making it painful to stand, let alone walk. It usually lasts about a week, sometimes more, sometimes less. Lupus is a beast. It's a battle, and the worst part is, you are fighting yourself, so if you win, you lose. Some days are better than others. I was fortunate that I had Elina to support and look after me. Dot too, but her support was punctuated by, 'So what exactly is wrong with you?'

Actually, *nothing* Dot. As I've explained many times. There is nothing to cure, it's auto immune.

'Can't you even get up? You don't look poorly.' *Oh, Dot!* Elina understood, and was immense in her efforts. Looking after the shop and looking after me. She took care of Rosie too, though I expect taking her out for a walk was a bit of a relief rather than a chore. Nobody else came to see me or got in touch.

Except Elliot.

He had my number, because I was weak and gave it to him and now he kept texting me.

C U @ Church????

On bike

No School!

Busy traffic.

Where R U

I didn't bother to reply, I didn't have the energy. It wasn't fair of me really, Elliot was okay. He had his problems too, I suppose. I think we were only friends because we were comrades in adversity, both victims and we sort of gravitated toward each other. Elliot was safe though, I'll give him that. And funny. I could trust him. If I need someone, not like now, but to talk to or hang out with, he is the most trustworthy boy I know, and I know quite a lot who aren't. He sort of reminds me of Rosie – or does Rosie remind me of him – whichever. They're both dogs. I mean that nicely. I love dogs, wagging their tails when they see you, desperate to please. He's like that.

I've had to be off all week and I'm bored. I am looking forward to going back to college on Monday just to break the monotony, even though I know what's waiting when I do. It's blonde and it's trouble, triple trouble.

Monday morning came, I felt okay. Well, okay enough to go to college. And, surprise, surprise, 'Oh look, it's loopy.'

'Have you been poorly dear?'

'Are you an ickle bit sicky then?'

Then peals of laughter followed by the, by now traditional, knocking of books out of arms. I spent most of the day trying to concentrate while being poked and pulled and whispered at. I really don't know how they're going to complete their education by spending so much energy on me. Anyway the bell finally rang for end of the day, we all gathered up our books and left. I made sure I was carrying a couple of books that they could cause me to spill. If I didn't it might force them to use their brains to think of something more creative to do, or am I giving them too much credit? I should have put money on it. As I reached the gates on my way out, there they were 'accidentally' bumping into me and laughing like donkeys as the books fell.

As I bent down to pick them up, I saw a pair of trainers by my head. 'Here, let me help?'

'What now?' I said. *Was that too loud?*

'Maeve. It's me.' I looked up.

'Elliot? What are you doing here?' He bent down to help me.

'Oooh, Loopy's got a boyfriend!' they sang, not even in tune. 'And he rides a bicycle, how sweet.' They turned and left, laughing.

'Sorry,' I said, 'Come on, just go.'

Elliot went to get his bike and I followed, 'Can I talk to you?' he said.

'Of course,' I replied, wondering what he'd have to say to me that was so important. 'But my Mum, Elina is waiting over there in our van.' He looked crestfallen.

'No, I can walk you home, but I wanted to talk to you.'

'It's actually quite a long way, you know.'

'I've got my bike, I can give you a crossbar.'

'What?' I started laughing. Elliot joined in.

'It's just – it's a nice day, and we're going the same way.'

'No we're not.' He *was* funny.

'Well sort of. It's really important.'

I thought for a moment, 'Alright, I'll check with Elina. Just a minute.' He gave me my books.

'Okay!'

I went over to where the van was parked, 'Hello, love. How are you feeling? Hop in,' said Elina cheerily.

'Er – no. I told Elliot we could walk home.'

'Walk! You've just had a week off, ill. What are you thinking of?'

'Elliot will be with me!'

'Elliot? The pastor's son?'

'Yes. I need the fresh air. I've been stuck indoors for a week.'

'I wish you'd let me know, I've come down here and sat in the van for nothing. What a waste of time. Oh alright then, I'll see you at home. Phone me if you need to, and I'll come and get you.'

'There's no need, it's only Elliot.'

'Oh alright then, if you insist.'

She drove off towards home and I went over to Elliot,

'So what did you want to talk to me about?'

'Your – condition.'

'What! You said it was important. Was that it?'

'Yes, for you, not me. You've been off all week and I've been texting.'

'How do you know I've been off all week?' He didn't go to the college.

'Well, I sort of pass by on my way to working at the centre and I haven't seen you.'

'Really?'

'Yes.'

'Is that where you're going now?'

'Yes.'

'How exciting, I've never been in there. Okay come on then. Can I have a go on your bike?'

'In a bit. It's not really safe here.'

That's what I meant about Elliot.

Safe.

THE BOOK OF ELLIOT

I've always felt different. Not biologically, but socially different. I get a bit awkward sometimes and find it hard to know the right thing to say, and when I'm pushed – when someone won't stop going on at me – I find it really difficult. My face starts to feel sort of full and my throat tightens up; then I need to release it all. Sometimes I cry. I know what it looks like and what they say, but it makes me feel so much better, and they stop pushing. Win – win!

I don't have a mother. I did once, but she died when I was young. People tell me endlessly about how brave and heroic my father is. They tell me endlessly how, if not for him, I might have died too. 'You must be so proud of him!'

As it was, I grew up hating small spaces and such, and my hands were a real mess compared to other people. I used to wear gloves most of the time, to protect me from infection and stuff, and to stop people looking and pretending they haven't seen. I'm no good at sports, I never have been. At school nobody wanted the weird kid on their side. Anyway, I didn't

131

like the macho attitude that seemed to always be there when it was games. Games are supposed to be fun aren't they? I enjoyed watching them on the TV sometimes. I could never catch or throw very well either, or hold bats or racquets. The best thing, for me, has always been my bike.

I cycle everywhere I can. Did you know, you can get from Cator Park in Penge, not too far from me, to either West Drayton one way – of course you'd have to get the train from Honor Oak to Colliers Wood, then the tube to Clapham High Street; then you can cycle all the way from there to the canal at West Drayton – or to Waltham Cross the other way? That would mean getting the train from Honor Oak to Shadwell, then Shadwell to Cutty Sark. From there you can stay on the cycle route all the way to Waltham Cross, through my favourite place: Freezywater.

Locally mind you, I do have to be careful where I leave the bike, especially at the end of the school day. I'm not at school any more. I left there years ago, thank God. Oh, perhaps I shouldn't say that, given who my father is. I still carry a puncture repair kit and a pump wherever I go, as I often find my tyres flat and school kids smirking round the bike racks, often singing 'Here comes Santa Claus,' then, 'Oh no! How did that happen?' they say; as wide eyed as it's possible to be without their eyebrows disappearing under their stupid fringes.

The names were as bad and the gloves didn't help. 'Don't like the cold, you little wus,' or 'little poofter.' I don't know where the 'little' came from because I'm average height. As for the rest, well, that's just stupid. There often followed a series of gay boy remarks, which I never understood but unfortunately seem to have been stuck with. I do remember, vividly, one time when it all got too much. A teacher was confided in, word got to the head, and an announcement was made about my hands. That solved nothing. One afternoon, the sporty types, who seemed to lead most of the 'fun', and their girlfriends, who encouraged them, decided that they wanted to see the scars for themselves. They took me behind the kitchen block, knocked me to the ground and they ripped the gloves off. When they actually saw my hands, they froze, just for a moment, then with faked regurgitation noises they left me there and ran off shouting,

'They're claws, they're not hands, he's got claws.'

Jokes started going around. 'Why doesn't Santa visit gay boy at Christmas? – Because he's got his own claws.' followed by, 'D'you get it? – Santa *Claws*!' And so, to everyone, I became Santa, and since then that was all that anybody ever shouted out. So that is how I seem to have become known. Amongst a certain section of society anyway.

I have been having operations since I was about five. I don't actually remember it happening, though I'm told it was a fire and my hands were burned. I only have a memory of pain and panic, but I can remember most of the operations. The hands have improved now, I suppose through time, growing and that. In fact you would hardly notice there was ever a problem. The scarring has all but gone, and mobility in my fingers is as good as anyone's. I still wear the gloves a lot of the time though, through habit, and probably always will.

It seems to have been taken for granted that I would work at the church when I finally left school. My father made sure I fitted in there and had plenty to do. There was a certain amount of training to be done, but that seemed to be 'for later'. In the meantime, I help with cleaning and putting out hymn books, orders of service, and other odd jobs that need doing. I have to study in the evenings, reading passages from the Bible that father chooses, and then answer questions on them over breakfast. Back in the day, I'd had absolutely no desire to remain at school a moment longer than was necessary, so as soon as I had finished the final exams, I left. I didn't even see out the term. I passed them all – some with distinction – so the path was clear for me to go to theological college eventually. The paperwork was a formality, and it was agreed – at least father had agreed – that I wouldn't start immediately; I would take some time 'in the real world' first. The 'real world' meant working at the church and the reiki centre, for very little. I can honestly say I didn't get it. Reiki that is. How can someone waving their hands over a person have any effect whatsoever? But, as the pastor's son, I had to at least be there at the clinic – sorry, centre – and if I was going to be there, I might as well use the time to find out what it was all about.

Strangely though, the pastor – I feel odd about calling him Dad – insisted on me taking a blood test every week. Nobody else had to. Perhaps he was concerned about me taking drugs or something, though he'd never had reason to be. I didn't mind. Anyway, as I said, I took an interest in what was going on. They said that when the place first opened and my mother ran it, that there were some amazing results, but since then not very much really. In comparison I mean. As I spent time there, I realised that people were actually getting a lot out of it and always seemed to leave with a lighter energy than when they arrived. People also reported improvement in their condition, whatever it happened to be, from cancer to depression. Maybe it was having a positive outlook that caused a physical effect, who knows? I continue to learn. I am told there are three levels to learning it. I'm on the first one, which involves opening the energy channels to connect the head, heart, and hands. You can even do reiki to yourself, which I find odd. There are books on the history of it all as well, which I have to read. All about Mrs Hawayo Takata, Chujiro Hayashi, and Mikao Usui; who started it all after meditating in the mountains of Japan, or something. I can't quite remember, but I'll look it up later.

Now I think of it, there were one or two *actual* cures that happened after I started there. Not because I started there, I hasten to add; I was little more than an observer at the time. Someone's migraines stopped happening and a woman said her little boy, who had ADHD and was causing havoc at school and at home, had started to be calm and attentive after treatment. It may have been coincidence, or possibly gratitude, but both the woman and the migraine sufferer seemed to spend a lot of time in and out of our house doing jobs for the pastor after their 'cures'.

I spent most of my days at the centre. I didn't have friends really, and not a lot to spend money on anyway. I had my phone and that was my main contact point with the world. I'm in a couple of WhatsApp groups, for the church and the centre; there's my cycling group of course and that's about it. Maeve texts with me now and then. It's mostly me to be honest. She's from the church, I mean I know her from the church. She goes to the healings with her mum. I'm not sure exactly what's up with her. There seems to be a lot of different things. I would like to get her to try the reiki treatment that we talked about, I'm sure it would help whatever she's got. I know I could help her. We don't get to talk or meet up much. I would very much like to see more of her and I'm sure she feels the same but, as I said, we text quite a lot. That was about it really, until that Sunday. Breakthrough!

My head was spinning, inside I was doing somersaults, I'd spoken to her. A proper conversation. All right I'd messed it up, made myself look a bit of an idiot, but I had done it, and she'd smiled at me. *At me!* I hardly noticed the traffic or heard the horns blasting all the way home. *She'd smiled at me!*

After that, I was like a guided missile, seeking her out at every opportunity. She was at the service again today, but had already left by the time I got away. I cycled home under a huge, dark, metaphorical cloud. The sight of the twin brick pillars that framed the driveway brought me back to Earth. The car wasn't back yet. I jumped off the bike as I went through between them, parked it in it's usual place just out of sight around the back of the house, and locked it. I hurried round to the back door, opened it and stepped into the sauna that was the kitchen. The aroma laden steam and the bustling, aproned woman that was Aunt Abigail greeted me cheerily as usual.

'Elliot! The hero returns from the fray. No doubt ravenous and ready to devour all before him?'

'Hi, er – yeah okay,' was my eloquent reply.

'Is your dad far behind you?'

'I don't know. There was some woman.'

'Is he bringing her back?'

When it was just family, the pastor disappeared into his study to prepare for the evening, and took his lunch with him. When there were guests, he blessed the dining room with his presence and the wisdom behind his twinkling smile warmed everyone.

'Dunno.'

'Well, there's enough. If not, I hope you're hungry! Is your bike away properly?'

'Yeah, yeah. Covered, tick. Chain, tick.'

'Right, go along then and get yourself ready. Two minutes!' I muttered my assent, and headed for the stairs.

'Take your shoes off, we don't want deposits of, who knows what, all over the house.'

I let out a sigh. 'Always something else, just relax will you.'

'Pardon?' called Abigail above the sound of vegetables rinsing under the tap.

'Nothing!'

I took off my shoes and pushed them under the dresser in company with various other pairs and went upstairs. Almost before I'd climbed the stairs Abigail retrieved them and tidied them, being careful not to disturb the carefully lined up footwear already there.

The scrunching of the gravel driveway told us that father had returned. Hopefully the bike was out of the way. The car door closed. Footsteps on the gravel, the door opened. I listened from the top of the stairs.

'On your own?' she asked.

'Yes,' came the curt reply, 'Why wouldn't I be?'

'No, it's just that Elliot said – '

'Elliot! What does he know?' He sniffed the air, 'I'll have a cold tray.'

He removed his shoes and put on a pair of house slippers, making sure his shoes lined up exactly where the slippers had been. Then without a look back walked through to his study. Abigail watched him go for moment. 'Hello, it's nice to see you too. How was the service? I'm so pleased.' Then she turned to the fridge and took out the cold meat slices. It only took a moment to prepare, as most of it was done already just in case, and Abigail carried the tray through. I heard the tap on the study door. There was no cheery 'come in' or even 'just a moment.' Not from him. Not a sound. Abigail went in and out again like a ghost. Not a word was spoken.

I came down the stairs back into the kitchen, just as the landline phone rang. Abigail went for it but father picked up the extension in his office almost immediately. We heard him say 'Ah, Mrs Greally, I need you tomorrow – yes I know but you'll just have to – '

The study door closed. I switched on my mobile as Aunt Abi plated the roast chicken, potatoes, cauliflower, and peas. It smelled fantastic.

'That will be the death of you,' Abigail said. 'You know he doesn't like it.'

'He's not here though is he?' I replied.

'You don't take your eyes off it, even on the stairs,' said Abigail. 'Anyway, it's rude to have a phone at the table. Switch it off again, and put it away.' This was Abigail attempting to put her foot down. She knew I wouldn't take a lot of notice.

'All right,' I said, 'I'll just finish this text.'

The world seemed to pause while she decided.

'Alright, but be quick – he could be in any minute and then you know what'll happen?'

I knew, but the rebel in me shrugged, and carried on for a moment longer, then I switched it off and tucked it into my sock; a habit I'd developed through my cycling adventures.

'Have you got any hand cream?' Abigail asked softly.

'Yeah, yeah,' I said a bit too sharply. 'Don't worry about it. I can look after myself. Anyway, I don't know what you're fussing about. I never use it, I don't need it any more.'

'Sorry,' said Abigail 'I – it's that I care about you. And you should look after your hands.'

'I know,' I said, whilst chewing through a juicy piece of chicken, 'This is nice.'

Abigail glanced down at my wrist, I pulled my sleeves down but she saw. She must have seen, but she said nothing. I should have taken the plaster off. Father insisted on the weekly blood test, he says kids of my age do drugs. *Kids, I'm twenty-one!* So he needs to take a sample and test it with his kit. He takes a needle and takes quite a lot. Then I stick a plaster on it, done! I don't know why he keeps doing it. I don't take drugs, I never have. It's been going on for the last couple of years, ever since my hands started to improve. He took a lot more interest in me then; perhaps he'd been ashamed of the scars, reminding him about Mum and what had happened.

It's Monday already. This week has gone past quickly. Nothing much has happened that's any different. I've cycled from church to centre and back again every day. I've been set the task of reading the book of Job in the old Testament; with a test every morning, naturally. It's all about how he kept faith despite all the terrible things that happened to him. Otherwise not much, except I have texted Maeve a few times, but she hasn't replied, I wonder if she's okay? Now that I know about her not being well, I think she may be having one of her 'things'. She said she had to lie down when that happened. I hadn't been out on my bike today and I thought, despite the forecast, it would be a good reason to get some fresh air. If she isn't well, she'd be at home, so I decided to take a ride out past their flower shop. I'd never been there so I had just checked the address and was setting out of the back door, when I heard the car pulling in. 'Damn!' I'd hoped to get away without any great long explanations, or any 'Just before you go, would you learn the first few chapters of Isaiah?' sort of stuff. As it happens, I do know Isaiah, it's all about children rebelling against their masters. Odd that should spring to mind.

It was too late, father was home. I didn't know where Abigail was though, she usually played left tackle for me when he was around – I have recently been watching some American football on the TV and left tackle seems to be the one who blocks anyone trying to hit the quarterback – I just thought it fitted.

'Elliot!' Ben shouted.

'Here we go,' I thought.

'I want you to get something for me from the centre.'

No, 'Please,' or 'Would you mind?' then?

'What is it? I was just going out.'

'I want some papers, they're on my desk, in the blue room, marked William Fillips.'

'I'll need the key then – please. I'll bring them back with me, I'm going out on my bike.' I waited.

'There, take these. Don't be too late. I need you to open up early tomorrow and I need to look at them beforehand.'

He passed me the keys, on a little key fob with a yin yang symbol attached to it.

'Okay!' I followed him back inside, then up to my room for my rucksack.

'Elliot!' he called. I stopped. 'Who made off with Job's oxen and donkeys?'

'The Sabeans,' I replied.

Then back out, onto the bike, and away. Freedom! I always felt like that on the bike. It was just me and machine, tearing through the streets and pathways of South London, with no-one to answer to, and the wind in my face. I felt alive.

It took about half an hour to get there. It wasn't on the main road, but just off it. As I pulled up outside, jumped off the bike and remembered to take off the cycle clips, I could see it was open; so I leaned the bike against the wall and made sure I locked it to something. There was a drainpipe outside so I wrapped the chain around that and went in. There was an elderly lady in the back of the shop, I could see her through the open store room door. I assumed it was a store room anyway. She was wearing a large colourful hat. I dinged the bell on the counter. She came into the shop with a nice professional smile.

'How can I help you, young man?'

'Oh, no – you can't really. I mean not for flowers at the moment, thank you.' She looked at me waiting. 'I wanted to know, er – is Maeve in at all?'

'Maeve? What did you want with her?'

'I haven't heard from her and I wondered if she was alright?'

'Well she's not here at this time of day dear, she's still at school. She doesn't like me saying that. College, she's at college.'

'Oh, I have been texting her, and she hadn't replied. I thought she might not be well or something.'

'No, no. She's well enough to go to college at least. I'm sorry I can't help any more than that. Come back later on, she may be home by then.'

I can't say I wasn't disappointed. Not that she wasn't well, but that she wasn't there.

'Which school – college – is she at?' I tried.

Of course, I knew where the college was, but I felt I wanted to be in that space, just a moment longer. This was where she lived.

'Oh, er now, it's the one on South Street, it's the secondary school, and it's the sixth form section. That's a bit of a tongue twister, South Street Sixth Form Section.' She laughed at her joke, which turned into a cough. I swear I saw her teeth move.

'Thanks. Funny,' I said, 'What time do they come out?'

'The usual school times, her mother has gone to collect her.'

'Oh, okay. When she comes back, could you tell her I came in?'

'Yes, yes I'll do that,' she started looking around, I suppose for something to write with. 'I'll just get a pencil from the back, I'm sure I had one. I answered the telephone here, but there was no message.'

She disappeared into the back. I waited. As I waited I thought, *South Street isn't so far, I could get there on the bike in ten minutes.* I checked my watch. A quarter past three. I could probably make it. Schools usually kicked out at somewhere between half past three and four. I called out to the back room.

'Never mind, I'll see if I can catch her later!' and I left.

The bike was still there. I know I hadn't been long, but one can never be sure. I turned the dial thing until the combination lined up. I won't say what it is, you never know. I jumped on and set off. I knew where South Street was. If I got a move on, I could be there in plenty of time. The traffic wasn't too bad; I only had a couple of near misses on the way, they may have been near, but they were misses nonetheless, so no harm done. When I got there I stopped just down along from the gates, where I could see, but I wasn't obvious. There was the flower van, parked up on the side street across from the school. I suppose people have to get there fairly early to find somewhere to park, as there were a lot of cars lined up and with their wheels on the pavement. Some with their engines running, so I must have made it just in time.

Then some of the younger kids started coming out, one or two together at first, but then momentum built from a slow stream into a flood. Kids of all shapes and sizes were jostling to get out through the narrow gates and, upon exiting, some took full flight as if fleeing for their lives. The older ones started walking through and I saw Maeve among them. I pushed the bike near to the gates so that she would notice me. She looked small. She had some tall, blonde girls close behind her. One of them bumped her and she dropped the books she was carrying; it didn't seem accidental, especially as the others were laughing and walking past her. I heard one of them say 'That was very rash of you, Loopy,' and her friend replied, 'Spot on,' to more laughter. I thought that was odd behaviour, but I had seen that sort of thing many, many times before and nobody was helping Maeve pick up her books; so I dropped the bike and knelt down beside her.

'Here let me help.'

Maeve looked at my shoes. 'No – I'm fine. Thanks.'

'Maeve, it's me – Elliot. I'll give you a hand.'

'Elliot!' She was surprised. Well of course she was, I didn't usually turn up out of nowhere to rescue her. 'What are you doing here?'

A fair question. 'I was worried about you. I've been texting and you haven't replied.'

The Blondes had stopped and were watching.

'Oh, Loopy's got a boyfriend,'

'And he rides a bicycle, how sweet.'

They turned and left, laughing.

'Who are they?' I asked.

'Just stupid girls in my year, take no notice of them.'

'Are they always like that?'

'Pretty much, anyway thanks. I've got to go, Mum's waiting.'

'Maeve?' I didn't really know what to say, I just didn't want the moment to end.

'Yes.'

'It's just that I hadn't heard from you,' I said lamely.

'I know,' she replied. 'I've been out of it a bit.'

'Out of it? What do you mean?'

I've not been well,' she went on. She obviously didn't feel she needed to explain. 'Oh, it's nothing new, it's just one of my – things. Happens from time to time. Look my mum's there in the van.'

I wanted to keep talking to her. I said, 'I need to talk to you. Can you walk home?'

'It's actually quite a long way, you know.'

Say something!

'I've got my bike.'

'What?' She started laughing. She has a lovely laugh. I joined in.

'It's just – It's a nice day, and we're going the same way.'

'No we're not.' She was still laughing.

'Well sort of. It's really important.'

Maeve thought for a moment, 'Alright, I'll check with Elina. Just a minute.'

'Who's Elina?'

'My mum, just a minute.'

I gave her both of the books that I'd collected, then she crossed the road and round the corner to where the van was parked. I waited with the bike and watched a very animated conversation take place. The van then drove off and Maeve came back empty handed.

'Okay, come on then, what is it that's so important?'

We started walking.

'Well, it's this thing of yours, the condition that you've got.'

She stopped. 'Is that it, you've come here specially to tell me I have a thing, a "condition"? Don't you think I hear enough about it at school, college, and all the rest of my, what you'd call, life!'

'Yes – I wasn't – I didn't mean – It's just that you come to the church and that, and I think it is working. Just, you mustn't give up.'

She walked on, head down. I'd upset her. That was the last thing I meant to do. After a minute or two of silence, she said,

'I did see your texts, but I've been feeling so ill that I really wasn't in the mood.' She seemed to make a decision. 'You see, it's this thing I live with. Lupus. I have to take pills and stuff to keep it quiet, but sometimes it flares up and it gets really difficult to cope. It's not a disease or a "condition" it's just the way I'm made. There is no cure. There's nothing to cure.'

'But you were at the healing again on Sunday. So there must be some hope?'

'Hope? Hope for what? Nothing will change. I just have to live with it is all, and with stupid people, like the clones just now.'

'The what?'

'Clones – identical people. All blonde, all tall, all self enti-tled, self obsessed, people, who think it's funny to kick other people that they look down on.'

'Sorry!'

'Yes. Everybody's sorry, but nothing changes. Nobody takes

a risk and stands up to them because they're just happy it's not them being picked on.'

This conversation had taken a turn I wasn't prepared for. I said, lamely, 'The church can help.'

Maeve let out an ironic laugh. 'That's Elina's idea as well. She thinks the sun shines out of your dad, and that a miracle's going to happen for me.'

'Well, it might. They say it has before, when my mum was alive. Perhaps it's because you don't believe it. Dad's always going on about faith and stuff, and if you believe enough, anything can happen.'

'So, now it's my fault. You see, that's the church. If it works they did it, if it doesn't it's your own fault.'

'Then why do you keep coming?'

This was met with a deep sigh, as if she was fed up with explaining herself. 'Elina likes to do the flowers for the services and I go with her. She believes it all and thinks any minute there'll be a miracle. Anyway, I work at the shop, and it will be mine one day I suppose. I have my future mapped out for me, so I'd better get back there and look after my inheritance.'

I really wanted to help, but I was quite powerless. I didn't even know what to say to her. She looked so vulnerable, so beautiful. Maybe one thing was the cause of the other. I've no idea which. I just wanted to be with her a bit longer.'

I'm learning the family business too.'

She laughed again, more openly this time. 'You're going to be a vicar?'

It should have been pastor actually, but I let that go.

'No. I'm working at the wellbeing centre. Learning how to do the reiki and other stuff.'

She glanced at me quizzically, 'New age "healing" for the rich and stupid.'

'I thought so too at first – kind of – but actually, it's not. I was doing a session the other day, there was this woman – client, we don't call them patients. It's really calm and peaceful, and it actually helped her to feel better.'

I didn't blame her for being a cynic. A lot of people were.

'What exactly is it then? What do you do?'

'It's a sort of massage – '

'Oh yeah? *That's* how you make extra money is it?'

'No – not that sort of massage, not like that. It can be a non-touching thing.'

'A massage without touching? What happens then? How does that work?'

'Well, it can be touching, but not always. There's candles – essential oil ones, so they smell nice – and your own choice of music.'

'I have to have massages for my lupus, I'd love "Bert Bedsprings" bouncing off the walls. That would relax me.'

'Who?'

'Springsteen! – There is no-one else.'

I didn't think that would work particularly. 'It's supposed to be calming really. Look, jump on the crossbar, it's not far. I'll show you.'

'What, I'm not getting on that.'

'Well walking will take longer. Anyway, why not take a risk then, step into the unknown. You may not think it's very safe, but it's fun and exciting.'

I held the bike out to her.

She gave in. 'Alright, how do I get on?'

We scrambled around for the best position. I got on first then she jumped and I hoicked, and off we went.

It wasn't far and it didn't take long but we were laughing. She was laughing and smiling with me! I don't know why it was so funny, maybe it was the shrieks and shouts and with one or two near misses involving pedestrians and some very hard looks, it actually became quite exciting. We were still laughing as we got to the centre. Maeve almost fell off the crossbar as we stopped and she went to the door.

'It's locked. There's no-one here.'

'No, not today. This is a recovery day when they see clients who can't get here.'

'I expect that costs,' she said then came away from the door and looked at the bike. 'Okay then, hold the bike while I get back on.'

'No, it's alright, I've got the key. I'm supposed to collect some papers for the pastor.'

'Do you learn all the massage stuff here then? You don't go to college for it?'

I had to admit it, 'I clean the place, as well as getting training. There's no official college course.' I unlocked the door and Maeve followed me inside. 'Welcome to the Hannah Saphan Centre for Wellbeing,' I announced.

'Hannah? Is that your mum?'

'Yeah,' I told her, 'They set it up together apparently and Dad named it after her when she died. It was really successful too, so they say, but then it kind of got a bit run down.'

'It looks nicer inside than out.'

'This bit is the reception area. We can't have it looking a dump, nobody would pay for that. Business has picked up over the last couple of years and there have been some actual cures.' *I must have some loyalty in me. Who knew?*

'From waving your hands over someone?' she asked. I wasn't sure if she was serious.

'Yeah, I know it sounds mad. But it's true.'

'I wish it were as easy as that. I'm stuck with this thing.'

I really liked her, and here we were alone, talking. I really wanted to help her.

'No, you'll become a famous scientist and find a cure, then you'll get rich flogging it.'

'Except, as I told you, there isn't one.'

I was showing her around the corridor; there wasn't much else really, just a few doors, and the cleaning cupboard. We went into the blue room, which was where father did his work.

Maeve was impressed, 'Wow, it's very clinic like, isn't it, and so tidy.'

'I know – because it is a clinic and I tidied it yesterday. This is the therapy room, that I work in sometimes.'

'Do you do reiki yourself then?' she asked.

I did a bit, but only as training. 'Yes, I'm learning it. I'm working on the first level,' I said. Well I was. She moved some files out of the way and sat on the table in the centre of the room.

'I've never really talked about it with anyone except Elina, but this lupus that I have. It's a real shit!'

I was a bit taken aback. She went on.

'You know they, some of them, call me Loopy at school.'

'I did hear that.'

'It's because of this. It's called Systemic Lupus Erythematosus. SLE or lupus, and it's for life.'

'You don't look ill,' I told her, trying to be supportive.

'Not today. But I have flare ups. It suddenly starts out of nowhere, then I feel sick, dizzy, my legs hurt, so I can hardly walk, and on and on. I have to take tablets all the time, massages every week, I've got to be careful what I eat. It goes on.'

'Is that why you've not been at school?' I asked,

'How do you know that?' she asked suddenly.

I felt caught, I wasn't a stalker. Well, I was, but only for good reasons. She mustn't think badly of me.

'I've been – well it's on the way from here – sort of – and I kept a look out.'

She looked at me strangely, and laid down on the treatment table. 'This is a bit firm. Right. Do it to me then.'

That was a surprise. 'What?'

'Give me a reiki.'

She looked fantastic.

'I can't.' It wasn't right, but could I pass up an opportunity like this, to get close to her.

'I thought you said you were training?' she said.

Alright then, I made the decision. 'The room needs to be dark and there has to be music and candles.'

'Go on then,' she encouraged.

So I hurried around, closed the blinds, and picked a couple of scented candles.

'Which do you want, lavender or patchouli?'

'Patchouli,' she replied with her eyes closed. Waiting patiently.

'Take off your jacket. You need to get comfortable.'

I went over to the CD player in the corner; there were a number of albums there, including a best of the '80s compilation, which had on it, surprise, surprise, 'Born in the USA'.

'Hey there is some Springsteen here.'

I wondered how she would react if I went a bit further.

'We may as well give this the best chance – can you take off your shirt?'

I held my breath. I loaded the CD and skipped through to the fifth track.

She asked, 'Er – do you really know how to do this?'

She had opened her eyes. Always reassure the client. Keep them relaxed. 'Absolutely, but I'm not so good at making it work through lots of layers.'

The music kicked in and I hardly heard the 'Okay.'

'Lie on your front and I'll just unclip your bra. I can't massage your back with it in the way.'

The smell of the patchouli was starting to make itself known; that, along with the loud music and the low light, was creating a heady atmosphere and kind of made it feel as if we were apart from the world. I hardly heard her say 'I hope your hands are warm.' They were, but so was the rest of me.

'It's alright. I know what to do.'

Except I didn't, I'd never had to deal with bras and the bloody strap wouldn't unclip. She laughed and sat up, then removed the bra completely. She was naked. I mean, her breasts were naked. Oh my God! They were pure and real and there, right in the open; I was shocked and excited all in the instant before she lay down again.

I put some warm oil on her back and rubbed it firmly across her shoulders and down her spine, then on the back of her legs.

'You are good at this, but don't get it on my skirt, it's the only clean one I've got,' she said softly. She lifted herself onto her elbows and looked round, 'I'd better slip it up a little.' She didn't see the effect she was having on me, 'Would you help?'

I carefully rolled the skirt up to her waist, but it wasn't going to work.

'Look it's easier if it comes off, do you mind?'

She shot me a warning glance but then shifted her weight so I could slip it down over her legs and off. I folded it and placed it on the chair. Then I went back to massaging her legs. How high should I go? She wasn't stopping me. She was relaxed, trusting. I rubbed her back. If I moved my hand low on her side, my fingers touched the curve that was her breast. It all became too much. I lost control, unzipped myself, then I couldn't stop. I turned her over, she yelped. I kissed her hard. I held those beautiful breasts. She seemed to freeze, though she felt soft and warm. Perhaps this was what it was like. She didn't push me away.

It was all over very quickly. In hindsight I may have been over eager and a little rough but I didn't appear to have hurt her. I hope not, because to be honest that hadn't crossed my mind, but she looked shocked. She didn't speak. I didn't know what to say. Then suddenly she let out this awful noise, as if she'd been underwater for ages and had just surfaced, grabbing at the air all at once. She gathered her clothes, put them on as quickly as she could, and ran out of the door.

I was stunned. What just happened?

'Shit! Fuck! Fuck! Fuck!'

What have I done? Oh My God. Was that – rape?

She hadn't said no, I hadn't meant to go that far, I just – couldn't stop myself.

I quickly sorted my own clothing and ran after her.

'Maeve!' I was shouting. 'I'm sorry, I didn't mean to. Maeve!'

But she'd gone.

THE BOOK OF REVELATION

'Oh well, a wasted journey really,' Elina said to herself. She was cross and hoped Maeve knew what she was doing. She was waiting to pick her up from school in the van as usual, but Maeve told her that she was walking home, with that boy. 'Boy indeed, he's almost five years older than she is. As long as it is just walking home, I suppose it's okay. He's the pastor's son, it's not some stranger that I know nothing about.' It was a long walk from the school to the shop especially with Maeve's problems. Elina was worried she might overtire herself and not be fit for anything the next day, but at least she wasn't on her own.

On the drive back home, Elina made a short diversion. She had taken the camera that Maeve had found into a photography shop and they had agreed to try and develop any pictures inside. With no guarantees, of course. Elina had the ticket in her purse, and she stopped outside on the double yellow lines. *Where could you go without those bloody lines everywhere?* she thought. She switched on the hazard lights. *Well, it doesn't count if you've got your hazards on, does it?* There wasn't anybody in the shop, and there was an assistant free. She handed in the ticket. The assistant went out the back and returned with a colourful envelope. Elina handed over copious amounts of cash, she didn't believe in plastic money, and dropped the photos, if indeed there were any in the envelope, into her bag. She had wanted to collect them with Maeve. She thought it might be an adventure they could share. She left the shop, waved at the snarling lorry driver struggling to get past her van in the traffic, and drove away.

Elina parked the van in it's usual place and went into the shop through the back door. As she entered, she heard the scrabbling of little doggy feet as Rosie heard her and came dashing to welcome her home. Perhaps she was just desperate for the toilet because she rushed through Elina's legs and outside to her favourite patch of grass. Elina picked up a bag and followed her out. Only after the necessary actions were completed did Rosie start jumping up trying to say hello. Elina checked her water bowl and made sure she had plenty of biscuits to nibble on. Then put on the kettle and started her daily routine at tea time, getting the meal ready. Which of course meant everything made freshly. Maeve's diet was tedious, but Elina loved her and nothing was a chore; when it was for her.

The shop bell tinkled suddenly, Elina smiled, but the heavy footsteps and the crying out of 'Mummy!' wiped it from her face. She dropped the knife and carrot she was peeling onto the floor and dashed toward the stairs, where Maeve collapsed against her, crying and exhausted, hardly able to draw breath. Rosie, too, ran out to her but stopped and backed off, looking quizzical.

'Maeve darling. What's happened?'

'Mu-um!'

'Come and lie down. Take your time. Shhh. It's alright. I'm here. I've got you.'

Elina held her tight, moving slowly to Maeve's room, and laid her down on the bed, still with both arms around her. 'There, it's alright. Now, just relax and tell me what's happened. I love you darling. Take your time.'

Maeve couldn't hold back any longer, the sobbing turned into something else, something primal. She gave herself completely to it. There was little Elina felt she could do, except be there, holding her, stroking her, until the storm passed.

Maeve slowly regained herself, though she still didn't move, save to hold onto Elina tighter. Terrified, but remaining as calm as she could, Elina said, 'There darling. I've got you. Whatever it is, I've got you. You're safe now. Can you tell me?'

Maeve was finding it difficult to catch her breath. 'Mum, oh mum.'

Elina looked at Maeve now and noticed that she wasn't dressed as she normally would be. *She's been running, out of breath, obviously she wouldn't be neat and tidy.*

'I thought you were with Elliot.'

'I was,' Maeve managed

'Didn't he help you?'

'It was him, Mum' Maeve sat up, her body rocking now.

'Him, what? What did he – Did he hurt you?'

'No – I don't. No!'

'Then what is it sweetheart. Please tell me. Then I can help you.'

Maeve stopped. Her world stopped, held as if in between

two moments, two minds. After an eternity she said, almost whispered, 'Elliot raped me. Elina, He – he – '

Then she crashed and the sobs took over.

'What? He did what to you?' Elina's face darkened.

Maeve could no longer speak.

'That boy. That boy did this to you. I will cut his balls off. He won't get away with this. I'm calling the police!'

She went straight to the phone in the living room. Maeve continued crying on her bed while Elina picked up the phone.

'It was all my fault, oh, I'm sorry.'

Elina was caught between calling the authorities and comforting her daughter. She dropped the phone and went back to her.

'No, don't ever say that. Look at the state of you. Nobody does that to you. You are not to blame. You hear me! You are not to blame!'

She didn't want to move away, she wanted to hold Maeve to absorb all the world's ills from her. She didn't even move to pick up the phone.

'Where is your mobile?'

Maeve pointed and Elina pulled it out of the rucksack and dialled 999.

Maeve was taken to the police station, with Elina. She gave a statement, she gave her clothes for examination, she gave samples. In exchange for dignity. The doctor was professional, but Maeve felt soiled. Maybe because she was professional. Maeve needed compassion.

The sequence of events at the centre had shocked her,

stunned her into inaction. Elliot was bigger than her, but he wasn't massive. She could have quite easily pushed him away or shouted something, anything, but she hadn't. The statement that she gave was a series of facts; cold, hard, indisputable facts. Her reactions and feelings were anything but. Did she lead him on? It wasn't the first time someone had touched her, though never like that. Questions went round and round in her mind. Elina was there with her every step of the way to support her and see that she was properly looked after. She had brought a change of clothes and was told not to allow Maeve to take a shower beforehand as it might destroy the evidence. They didn't need evidence she thought. She had told them what had happened.

After a few hours, Maeve and Elina were driven home; attended by a nice WPC, who made sure they were settled at home and gave her a personal phone number, 'If there is anything I can do. Please call me at any time. Day or night. Even if you just want to talk.'

Across town, another police car sped on its way. It screeched to a stop and two uniformed police officers got out. They went and knocked on the door. Abigail opened it.

'Good evening Ma'am. Does an Elliot Saphan live here?'

'Why yes,' she said, 'What on earth could you want him for?'

The police officer continued, 'We need to speak with him ma'am if you wouldn't mind.'

Ever mindful of prying eyes, Abigail invited the two officers inside and into the kitchen. She picked up a chair from the floor and set it on its legs again. She called up the stairs.

'Elliot! Come downstairs please.'

She waited. 'Now!'

Ben appeared from his study. 'Good evening Officers, how can we help you?'

The first police officer repeated himself.

'Are you Mr Elliot Saphan, sir.'

'I'm his father, what has he done?'

'We're not at liberty to say just now sir,' said the second officer.

Elliot appeared at the foot of the stairs. On seeing the police in the kitchen, the blood drained from his face. The four people turned toward him, with differing expressions on their faces.

'Are you Elliot Saphan?'

'Y-yes, I am.'

'We need you to come with us to the police station sir. A serious complaint has been made concerning you, and we need to talk to you.'

Ben jumped in, 'What kind of complaint. What's he done? Can't you talk here?'

'Again, we cannot say at this stage sir.' Then to Elliot, 'We need you to come with us sir.'

'I demand to come with him. I'm his father. I have every right.'

'On the contrary sir, Mr Saphan – '

'Elliot!'

'...is an adult sir. You may come to the station separately of course, but for the moment Mr Elliot Saphan needs to come with us.'

Abigail took a step toward Elliot.

'Oh, Elliot. What's happened?' she pleaded.

Elliot looked at the ground and walked to the door. One of the officers took his arm and helped him down the steps and into the waiting car.

∾

Much later that night, Elliot was released on bail pending further enquiries. But what was bothering Elliot now, were the further enquiries being made by Ben and Abigail.

'Rape!' Ben shouted. 'Rape!' As if he hadn't heard the first time.

'No, it wasn't like that,' pleaded Elliot, looking as if he didn't know what had hit him. 'I thought it was okay.'

'Okay. Just when has rape ever been okay?'

'She didn't stop me, I mean I had never meant anything, but it just happened.'

Abigail was almost in tears, 'Who is she, this poor girl?'

'Maeve. Maeve Lucas. Her mum's got a flower shop,' Elliot almost whispered.

'She's one of the parishioners who comes to the healings, she has some condition or other. Her mother does the flowers. They own a shop not too far from here,' said Ben.

Abigail continued, 'How is she? Did you hurt her? Because if you did, so help me.'

'No-no-no, I would never hurt her – we're friends.'

'Not any more!' Ben jumped in. 'How is this going to reflect on us, on the church, the centre? Do you know what you have done?'

'I didn't do anything wrong – not on purpose.'

'Oh, rape is not wrong? How the hell can that be by accident?'

'Did you say she came to the healing services?' Abigail said quietly.

'Yes she had some thing. She called it lupus,' whimpered Elliot.

'Ben,' she continued, 'We need to talk. Now. Elliot stay here and just think. Think hard about what you've done.'

'That's it? That's the extent of it? He brings everything crashing down around us and all you've got is "Think about what you've done"?' Then to Elliot, 'Do you know what they do to rapists?'

Abigail took Ben's arm. She had never laid hands on him in anger in her life. Ben was surprised. She said, 'He's not the only one capable! I haven't forgotten. Come out.'

Elliot went upstairs and slumped onto his bed. Ben followed Abigail out of the room.

'What the hell is that supposed to mean, and what is it that is so important?' he hissed.

'She is ill, and Elliot had sex with her.'

'Yes, we know only too well.'

'Ben, stop being angry and think. She goes to healing, and Elliot has had sex with her. She won't need to go to healing any more, will she?'

It took Ben a moment, 'My God! Elliot had sex with her!'

'And Elliot hasn't been told about his history.' Abigail looked at Ben and continued, 'What do we do? It can't get out, not like this. Elliot's not ready.'

'Elliot will never be ready,' replied Ben.

'That's not fair Ben. He needs to know.'

'No!' Ben suddenly looked under pressure. He was suddenly urgent. His eyes moving rapidly. 'I'll deal with her.'

'Her?' said Abigail.

'It – it, the situation. I'll deal with it,' he hurried down the stairs 'It's under control.'

Abigail followed, 'How? How can it be under control?'

Ben was very agitated, 'A girl from the church, let the church deal with it.'

Abigail stopped outside the study, more from custom than thought. She never went into the study unless with a meal. She said, 'He's been texting her.'

'He's been what? Texting! Why didn't you tell me? We said no! No girlfriends.' Ben turned, furious now. 'We agreed!'

For the first time in a very long time, Abigail stood up to him. 'No. You agreed. I thought it was innocent enough.'

'Well it's obviously not, is it. If it all comes out there'll be trouble. He'll be "Miracle Boy" or some such and there will never be peace. I knew it! I knew it!' he continued, this time shouting up the stairs at Elliot, 'What the hell have you done? The Police coming to the house, how does that look? Raping a girl.'

He started to climb back up the stairs. 'Where was it, hey? In the centre? In my room?' Ben entered the bedroom. Elliot stood up. 'Going to show me, were you? Well I'll show you!' Ben swung his fist toward Elliot but missed.

'It has to be from God. God is the only way. God heals. God sends the spirit to us. Not some spotty teenager.'

Abigail had run upstairs behind Ben.'

'Calm down Ben. Trust him. He's old enough.'

'Alright, you're old enough are you, well here it is. Elliot, you were always going to be told. The healing. It's you. Not the church, not the healing services. Not the centre. It's all you. It's in you just like your mother. She had the power to heal in her blood. It was passed to her and she has passed it to you, you are her firstborn, and you have thrown it in the face of God! Do you think God wants rapists? Genesis 34:29. The sons of Jacob plundered the city, because their sister had been defiled. They took their sheep, their oxen, and their donkeys, what was in the city and what was in the field, and all their wealth. All their little ones and their wives they took captive; they plundered even all that was in the houses. Now you, Elliot Saphan have defiled a sister and our city, our very lives, will be spoiled and plundered. All will be taken from us. You have destroyed my Church.'

Abigail tried to stop his outburst. 'Ben, no. Not like this.' Elliot was almost crouching in fear. He cried, 'I don't understand! I haven't done any of that. I love her!'

'Love her. You don't know the meaning of the word!' screamed Ben, right into Elliot's face, forcing him to turn away.

Abigail tried to explain. 'Elliot, your hands were dreadfully burnt, and for years you had to live with it and for that, I'm sorry. So sorry. But when you matured, they started to get better.'

'No,' said Elliot, 'it's because of the operations and the creams.'

'No, Elliot.' Ben was calming down now, 'The healing at the services and at the centre. It was because they were given some of your mother's blood. Now that you have grown, they were given yours.'

Elliot was beyond surprise now, 'My blood, but how did you get my blood.'

Abigail suddenly realised, 'The drug tests! They weren't for drugs at all. They were for you.'

'Everyone loves you because of me. Because you used *my* blood!'

Ben was different now. Cold, dangerous.

'This girl, Maeve Lucas, will know, and her mother will know; then everyone in the whole world will know. Look, nobody really believes God can heal like that, but they have faith. And a miracle? If it happens once or even twice, even in a small way, may not get people to flock to the church, but it will make them curious. Some will be sceptical. As in Jesus's own lifetime they will say, "They weren't really healed, it's all a set up, they weren't really ill in the first place." However, it does encourage faith. That it might just happen again. They have hope, and the church will thrive, we will thrive. But if they know it's you, and they know it's a real miracle. First there will be a few, then there will be many. Then we won't be able to turn around, to breathe, for the hordes of people that want you to – to just touch them.'

Elliot looked as if his world was caving in, 'You lied to me. All this time. Both of you. They laughed at me, and you lied and lied and lied. You could have said, you could have told me.'

'No, Elliot, you were too young.' Abigail tried to be so gentle.

'Too young,' said Ben, 'Too weak you mean.'

He turned, went down the stairs, picked up his briefcase from the study, and without a word left the house. While Abigail held Elliot's head and he sobbed in her lap, they heard the familiar engine fire up and leave.

Ben was possessed by an urgency, a need. The reputation of the church was at stake. His reputation was at stake. If he didn't fix this, it would all come out: the fire, the deception, Hannah. Everything would be over. He would lose it all.

He knew the address of the shop, he'd been paying the flower invoices for a long time; the streets were relatively quiet at that time of night, though there was some traffic about.

There was always traffic about, so it was only a few minutes before he arrived. He pulled up outside, jumped out of the car with his black briefcase and hammered on the door. Lights came on upstairs and he heard the feet thumping on the stairs and a dog barking. The door opened.

'I have just heard what happened. How is she? There is no time to lose,' Ben said, all in a rush, pushing past Elina as he spoke.

'She's – what? Upstairs. She's very upset. I don't think you should be here. She can't be – ' Elina followed, trying to get in front of Ben to stop this human tornado.

'She has suffered a terrible trauma at the hands of my son. I am here in the name of a righteous God to right that wrong, and take away her affliction.'

Ben climbed the stairs with Elina behind in a fruitless attempt to keep up. Rosie was barking and running in circles. He continued, 'I have been compelled to come here to take the pain away in His holy name. I know she has suffered and has been suffering for some time. Now is the time that the Lord has called her name.' Rosie's barking was relentless. 'It is to end,' then suddenly, 'Where is she?'

Elina was overwhelmed, 'In there but – Rosie, Rosie stop it!' Elina picked Rosie up, pushed her into the kitchen and closed the door. It didn't stop her.

The bedroom door flew open as Ben pushed and Maeve sat up, blinking, confused at the sudden intrusion. In a commanding voice Ben started.

'Come, pray with me. Pray for the Holy Spirit to enter her soul and cleanse her.'

He planted his feet astride the rug, laid one hand on Maeve's head, the other reaching for the heavens and cried 'Lord I am here to do your will. It is as you have commanded. In the name of The Father, the Son, and the Holy Ghost. Depart thee disgusting disease from this poor sinner.'

'Rosie!' Maeve called, 'Elina, where's Rosie?'

Elina looked on. She had to stand behind Ben in the small room. She found her voice again. 'She's in the kitchen,' then to Ben, 'It's your son is the sinner.'

Ben took no notice of her and continued, 'Cast these demons from her into the depths of hell.'

'*Our Father*,' he gestured for them both to join in. He opened the briefcase and took out a small bottle.

'Which Art in Heaven
hallowed be thy name;
thy Kingdom come;'
He poured some of the liquid into a shot glass.
'thy will be done;
on earth as it is in heaven.
Give us this day our daily bread.
And forgive us our trespasses,
as we forgive those who trespass against us.
And lead us not into temptation;
but deliver us from evil.
For thine is the kingdom,
the power and the glory,
for ever and ever.
Amen.'

He made the sign of the cross over the glass and planted his hand firmly on Maeve's head, forced it back, and made her drink. Maeve, in shock, complied.

Ben collapsed onto the floor breathing heavily and sweating profusely.

'Now you are in the presence of the Lord in a holy place. You must be penitent and ask forgiveness for your trespass and forgive the sins of others.' Suddenly he shouted, 'Do it! Now!'

Elina was forced to comply. 'We beg your forgiveness Lord.'

Maeve had no idea what was going on. 'Mum?'

'Say it!' demanded Ben.

'We beg your forgiveness,' she said.

'And forgive others their sins against us. Say it,' said Ben a little gentler this time.

'And forgive others their sins against us,' they said in unison.

Ben let out a huge sigh of relief and said 'If God speaks truly in his promise to us; Maeve Lucas, your affliction is no more. Get up. Go. Test yourself – Go!'

He sat on the end of the bed with his head in his hands. Rosie finally stopped yelping. Neither of them dared say a word. Elina and Maeve looked at each other.

'Go, go go!' repeated the minister.

Then Maeve climbed out of the bed, trying not to kick the pastor in doing so. They left the bedroom, and pulled out the home testing kit that was kept in the kitchen drawer, releasing Rosie as they did so. She immediately rushed to Maeve's bedroom to confront the intruder and stood guard, growling at him. With hardly a word spoken – they had been through this procedure countless times – Elina and Maeve went through the motions of taking a little blood and putting it in the solution, mixing it well, and putting some drops in the receptacle.

'While we're here would you like a drink?' asked Elina.

'No mum. What is going on?'

'Do you think he'd like one?' Elina went on, trying to be the gracious host. Never mind the circumstances, one must have good manners.

'Who knows?' said Maeve.

They sat quietly together for a minute or two, listening to Rosie's noise, then completed the procedure by placing it into the envelope ready for posting first class the next morning. They weren't quite sure what to do next. The pastor was in the bedroom. There was nothing more to do. Elina went in to him, picked up Rosie and said, 'Er – we've done the test.'

He looked up. He looked very hot and red in the face. 'And?' he barked.

'We don't know, we have to send it to the lab and wait for the results,' she replied, taken aback a bit by his rudeness.

'The Lord has been here today and has done his work.'

Now Maeve was standing outside the open door behind Elina. Ben was speaking to her, 'Now, rest my dear girl and forget about all this terrible business, as if it never happened. It has brought about your healing. You have been blessed. Be penitent. We don't want to make a liar out of our Lord now do we. Forgiveness is the cure. Rest. As if it never happened. Never!'

'But we have to wait, as I said,' Elina insisted.

'Very well. We'll see. We'll see. Faith is the answer. Let me be clear. There has been a miracle here today. The Lord has cured her,' he said. Then he stood up, satisfied, relieved, and replaced the bottle and glass in the briefcase; then left the way he had come.

Elina handed Rosie to Maeve, followed him down the stairs and locked the shop door behind him. Maeve watched from the window as the car drove away into the darkness. Elina came back upstairs and shepherded Maeve back into the living room. She plonked herself down on the sofa, but kept hold of Rosie, who was desperately licking her face and looking for praise for the great job she had done in seeing the intruder off, and Elina carried on into the kitchen.

'I can't go back to bed after that,' Maeve said, 'I feel as if I've survived a tornado. Though I'm not sure I did survive. Elina, what just happened?'

'Take a breath love,' Elina said from the kitchen, over the sound of the kettle heating up and her still racing heart. 'Do you want a drink?'

'Yes, please. Anything.'

Elina made the tea and brought the cup in. She wanted to distract Maeve, take her mind off all that had just happened. They sat together in silence for a minute. 'Oh, I picked up those photographs from the shop. Do you think we dare have a look?'

'I'm too stressed at the moment. It's ten o'clock at night.'

'Forget tomorrow, we'll take the day off. We'll just have the day to ourselves. I'll put a notice on the shop door.' Elina was speaking in a soft calming voice.

'Can we? Really?' said Maeve. She relaxed visibly. 'Alright then,' she carried on, 'Everyone loves a mystery, right?'

Elina went to get her bag. She rummaged around in her bottomless shoulder bag, and pulled out an envelope. 'Look,' she said, opening the flap. 'Just as I told you, it has an extra little pocket, with all the photo negatives in.' She brought it back in to show Maeve, but Maeve had closed her eyes. Elina smiled to herself – perhaps it's for the best – and she put the packet on the sideboard. 'Come along,' she said 'This can all wait 'til the morning. Let's get you back in bed.'

Maeve allowed herself to be led back to bed, just like the little girl she used to be. Rosie leapt down and followed her proudly. Elina tucked them both in and went back to finish her tea. *What on earth was the pastor thinking?* She admired him a great deal, almost hero worship at times, but this was very strange behaviour. Hands on support for parishioners was one thing, but so late in the evening? And to burst in like that with a full on, almost exorcism. Could she be cured?

Her gaze fell on the envelope. Out of curiosity she picked it up and spilled the contents onto the table. There were quite a few pictures, mostly blurry ones of Rosie but only three others, and 6 strips of negatives. She picked up one of the strips and held it to the light, it was blank. There were no pictures at all. The same was true of the others, apart from the pictures of Rosie, except one. The camera must only have been used three times. She paid a lot of money for three old photos. She took them out of the envelope. The first one was a baby; the next one brought back a lot of memories, it was Devon with Maeve in a park. She hadn't seen Devon or any image of him since he left all that time ago. It affected her more than she wanted to admit. She wondered where he was and what had happened to him over the years. The third one was Maeve again, but with a young woman. *Was that Maeve's real mother?* No it couldn't have been, Devon was there.

'Is it Maeve?' she said aloud. Elina went to a box in the bottom of her wardrobe. It was full of photo albums, old bills, documents no longer relevant, and the adoption papers that gave Maeve to them; with the child's photo still clipped to the top. She took the papers into the living room and compared them with the photo on the table. That baby was definitely Maeve. In fact she was wearing the same clothes in both pictures. That was odd, because Elina bought a whole load of completely new clothes as soon as Maeve arrived. And, where was that park? She was sure she'd never been there, and nor had Devon, at least not with Maeve. Come to think of it, they hadn't had a pushchair like that either. Elina was too tired, her mind must be playing tricks on her. She'd get some sleep and look again tomorrow, and try to make sense of it all. She tidied up the pictures and put the negatives back in the envelope with them. Then she put them all together in her bag and went to bed.

~

In the morning Maeve was first up, 'Hola, Alexa. Por favor, encienda la radio.' She danced into the kitchen and put the kettle on for Elina. Rosie was happily running in circles round her legs causing Maeve to laugh out loud. Elina came out of her room, more closely resembling the living dead.

'Hola Alexa, baje el volumen a la radio por favor!'

'Kettle's on, good morning!' greeted Maeve cheerily.

'What on earth's got into you this morning?' grumbled Elina, suffering from the effects of the night they'd had.

'I just feel – great!'

'You obviously thrive on very little sleep, but I don't,' said Elina sitting down on the sofa. 'And give that little ball of cotton wool something to eat. Stop her running around like a whirlwind.'

'I will, just as soon as I've taken her outside. Come on Rosie!'

Maeve, followed by Rosie, went downstairs and out of the back door to give the little dog a chance to relieve herself. While she stood there waiting, Maeve breathed in the morning air. Despite the bins nearby and the traffic a hundred yards away, she felt good. She hadn't felt like this for – ever. Then she called Rosie and they both bounded up the stairs. Rosie went straight into the kitchen and stood by her bowl waiting. Maeve dealt with her, then made herself her usual morning green tea. Elina dressed and spent a little time in the bathroom, transforming herself from a zombie into a presentable human being, before going to the kitchen to start breakfast.

'I was meaning to stay in bed a little longer this morning, after last night. How are you feeling?'

Maeve turned to look Elina squarely in the eyes. 'I – feel – great! I've never felt this good.'

'I know it'll take you a while to see things clearly, after the – assault. I understand that, and I'll give you all the space and support you want. This is probably some kind of reverse reaction to the events of last night, or something. Take it easy love. How are your legs today?'

'Fit and ready to run! Did it happen? Is it true? Was there a miracle here last night?' she said excitedly.

'Miracle? I think it's a little early for that Maeve. It's more than likely adrenalin from last night. Shall we wait for the test results before we start the hallelujahs? In the meantime, shall we try a little breakfast?'

'Yes, yes I will. You're wrong though you know, I can feel it. He was right as well.'

'Who was right? About what?' said Elina, puzzled.

'The pastor. We should forgive. I know what Elliot did was awful, and I hated him for it, but I've been thinking hard about it, and perhaps some of it may have been my fault.'

'No,' said Elina vehemently. 'It's not your fault. None of it was your fault, and that boy should get everything that's coming to him. Don't even think it was any fault of yours. Maeve. Look at me. It was not your fault!'

'We should forgive. Like he said. Especially now.'

'Yes we should forgive, but it doesn't mean letting people get away with the evil that they do. Just retribution, along with forgiveness. That's what we need. Let the authorities deal with him. Then when he's safely locked away and can do no more harm. Then we can forgive.'

'I can't help the way I feel today. I'm going to have a full fry up, with everything on.'

'Now, now.' Elina tried to calm things down, 'Let's not go mad. Wait for the result and then go mad, or not. Anyway we don't have fry up things in the house.'

'All right, but we do have tap water.' Maeve picked up a glass and filled it from the tap, then looked at Elina and drank it straight down. 'And a proper cup of tea, with milk.' She switched the kettle on again.

Elina sighed, 'If you must, then. If you're feeling so good, you can take Rosie out for a bit of exercise.'

The kettle didn't take long to boil and Maeve made the tea. 'And,' she hesitated, 'And I'm not taking any meds today!'

'What?' Elina almost burst. 'Now, you listen to me, changing your diet is one thing. You're the one who's going to suffer, but those meds are important. They affect both of us. Don't forget, I'm the one who has to pick up the pieces.'

Maeve tried to stand her ground. 'Didn't you hear what he said last night? Faith. You have to have faith. Well I know. It's gone. It worked. I'm cured. I am finally rid of it all.'

'Maeve, please. I appreciate your excitement and your euphoria, but wait. Please, please wait. Don't risk your health, for – an idea. Please wait for the tests.'

Maeve could see the worry in Elina, the real hurt she was feeling, 'Okay Elina,' she said softly, 'I'll wait for the test, but then you'll see. God was here.'

Maeve went to the bathroom for the meds that she had to

take every day, usually just to stay on a level with the world. Elina called 'I'm sorry, love, but it is for the best, believe me.'

'I know,' replied Maeve, rattling the pill bottle so that Elina heard, then putting it back in the cupboard. She drank down a small glass of water, from the tap again, and then came out. 'Come on Rosie,' she tickled the little dog, 'Let's go and have some fun.'

They left the shop to find a bus that would take them to Leaves Green, only a few stops away where Rosie could run to her little heart's content. Where Maeve could take in some fresh air and greenery. Where with space around her, God's natural world, she could think. She felt odd, lighter and free, but with a touch of fear. *What if it wasn't true?* The bus came, she picked Rosie up and got on.

Elina watched them go, she was worried about Maeve. Whenever someone reaches a high like that, the crash back down to earth is going to hit hard and soon. Now was a perfect time to have a good look at those papers. She went and collected the adoption papers from where she left them in her bag, and pulled the photographs back out of the envelope. She compared the photos again. There was no mistake. It was the same baby girl. Elina knew that the adoption society wouldn't give out the natural parent's names, especially over the telephone, but she hoped she might get some information. Dates, places, anything really. She rang the number on the paper. 'South London Adoption Society,' the voice answered. 'My name is Serena, how can I help you?'

'Ah, hello, my name is Elina Lucas. I and my husband, that is my husband at the time, adopted a baby girl through your agency about just over sixteen years ago, er – 2006. I was wondering if you could access the records for me.'

'I'm afraid, we can't give out that sort of information, certainly not over the phone,' said the voice that was Serena, helpfully. 'I could check your details for you though. What is your name?'

'My name is Lucas, Elina Lucas. My husband's name was Devon.'

'I'm so sorry, I'll have a look.'

'Sorry? Why are you sorry?' puzzled Elina.

'Did your husband die? Is that part of your inquiry?'

'No.' Elina almost laughed. 'He might as well have. Divorced, quite a while ago.'

'Oh.' Serena was embarrassed now, 'It's just, when you said was, I assumed. I am sorry.'

'Never mind,' Elina carried on, wanting to get back to the subject, 'Devon and Elina Lucas.'

'Date of birth?'

'Me or him?'

'Both if you are able.'

'I can give you mine,' she said.

Elina answered all the identifying questions that seem to be part of every official conversation these days and, being satisfied, Serena said, 'Hold on one moment.'

Elina waited, listening to the radio in the background competing with the distorted holding music on the phone. She got fed up with it. 'Alexa, por favor apaga la radio!'

'Hello? Is that Mrs Lucas?'

'Yes I'm here.'

'I'm a senior advisor here at the SLAS and I'm pleased to say we do have your records archived here still, from your enquiries in 2006.'

'Yes,' said Elina, 'And you found us a beautiful baby girl.'

'Well, there seems to be a problem with that. There is no record of any adoption through us.'

'There must be some mistake,' Elina answered.

'Are you sure you have the right agency? This is the South London Adoption Society.'

'Yes, of course. I have the paperwork here, in my hand.'

'Do you have any reference numbers by any chance?' She was being patient.

'Yes, here at the top. SLAS DL100506G.'

'I'm very sorry, but that doesn't match our reference format at all. The best thing would be if you were to make an appointment to come in and see us. I'm sure there is something we can do to clear this up.'

An appointment was made for the following week and Elina replaced the receiver, even more puzzled than before. She went back through the living room into the kitchen, dropping the papers on the table on her way. She made another cup of tea. There wasn't much to do when the shop wasn't open except, perhaps, tidy up downstairs and get some of the orders ready. It was nice to know that she wasn't going to be disturbed by customers. She could relax. Take her mind off things.

She took the tea downstairs and got on with some paperwork. One of the things about flowers, though, is that you mustn't prepare too early, or they wilt. So, even though a big wedding was coming up in a month's time, nothing could be done yet. She could get on with ordering the churches flowers. The church was one of her oldest customers, and it had become routine. Dot had been told not to come in. She was grateful. The years had been good to her, but she was beginning to feel her age now; so an extra day off, with pay of course, would do her good.

Maeve came back around lunchtime, eating a sandwich.

'What are you doing?' Elina said as soon as she saw her, 'You know what that might do to you.'

'I told you, it won't. I feel so free. It's amazing how the simplest of things can make you feel.' She tore off a corner and dropped it to Rosie, who had been pulling at the lead in a hurry to greet Elina.

'I was going to get you lunch.'

'Thank you, but I'm fine with this. I'll take Rosie up and give her hers.'

Ben had gone to the church. He was happier. The rage in him seemed to have dissipated over the last few days. He was in control again. Although there still remained the problem of how to keep all this out of the newspapers. It wouldn't do for a pastor's son to be in the news for anything negative, let alone criminal, and this was the worst kind of criminal. Elliot had been very upset, understandably, and had become completely reclusive.

Abigail was in the house, cleaning as usual and tidying. Elliot had locked his door, as he seemed to do a lot these days, so she couldn't go in to him. She desperately wanted to comfort him, tell him it would be all right, but she didn't know that it would be. He wasn't her child, but she didn't want to lose him. She owed it to Hannah. She made herself a cup of coffee. Not the instant, she hated the instant; she had a machine that you had to put, what they called, a pod in. You know the ones, advertised by that actor. It was a bit noisy, but it was quick, mess free, and the coffee tasted fantastic, easily as good as cafe coffee she thought. When it was brewed, she went into the spacious lounge to watch the morning news, and sat down in her armchair. It was a bit old fashioned, with fringed brocade all round, but it was comfortable and had a small footstool for that extra luxurious feeling. She put the china coffee cup down on the Queen Anne table beside her and reached down for the TV remote, which was in the side pocket of the armchair, and she pressed the power button. The adverts came on. She switched channels to get the headlines. The chancellor had done something stupid, there were some unhappy workers talking about strikes, there was somebody had been stabbed. She dropped the coffee cup and screamed. The victim's picture had come onto the screen. It was David. It had been a long time, but it was him! There was now a great brown stain on the rug and a broken saucer, but – David! They were saying they needed the public's help in identifying him. There was no mistaking him. He looked worn, tired, but it was him.

She hurried to get a cloth and some water. What was it 'Good Housekeeping' said about coffee stains? Washing up liquid and white vinegar she thought. She started mopping it up with the cloth first, whilst listening to the report. It was only short and she had missed most of it getting the cloth. She turned the channel back to ITV. It wasn't long before the report came on, these morning programmes can be a bit repetitive. It was David! The report said he had been stabbed in South London, and police were still trying to identify the assailant. They needed information about David, or this unidentified man, and his attacker. There was a number to ring with any information. She didn't know who attacked him, but thought getting his name right might be a useful bit of evidence. She had thought of David often. She had thought of Rebecca constantly.

177

She called the number and left all her personal information, along with her bit of evidence, and how she knew him. That was that. She felt that she ought to do more, go somewhere, tell someone else, something. But there was nothing she could do. There was a stabbing reported at least every other day nowadays, and this one wouldn't make the headlines for very long. She wondered what he had got mixed up in. She was more shaken than she thought.

That afternoon, the phone rang. The landline that is. 'Hello, could I speak to a Miss Abigail Derzel please.'

'Speaking.'

'Good afternoon, this is PC Hammond, the duty officer at Scotland Yard response centre. I believe you called our information number earlier today, regarding an image broadcast on TV,' said the voice.

'Yes, I did. To be honest, I don't know if it would be any help or not; there was a picture of someone that I know, I mean, knew some time ago. But they didn't know his name.' She waited.

'I see, and are you certain about this man. Do you have any documentation?' continued the voice.

'I'm sure I can find something. I almost didn't hear it properly I was so shocked by the picture.'

'What name did you know this person by?' asked the voice.

'His name is David Lawrence, I knew him very well about fifteen years ago. He was the father of my daughter.'

'Thank you, and you are absolutely certain that it is the same man?' the voice pressed.

'Absolutely,' Abigail said, 'It wasn't a very good picture, but there is no doubt.'

The voice on the phone continued, 'Thank you very much,

Miss Derzel. I think we may need to talk to you further about this. Would you be free this afternoon, if we were to send a car to fetch you?'

Abigail hesitated, Ben would not like another police car turning up at the door. 'Would it be possible, that the car not come to the house? Could it pick me up away from here, you see my brother-in-law wouldn't like – '

The voice interrupted her. 'Of course madam, could you tell me your address and postcode? Then I can arrange for you to be met at the nearest police station to you.'

She gave him the details and he came back very quickly with, 'It will be Bromley Police station, on the high street, Bromley. Post code BR11ER. If you could go there and make yourself known at the front desk, an officer will be with you to discuss this further. Would you take any information that you might have, relevant to – ' he consulted his notes, 'Mr Lawrence, along with you please.'

'Should I go now?' she asked.

'At your convenience madam, but the sooner the better really. I'll be in touch with them now. Thank you,' he said before ringing off.

David. It had been a long time. When she met David it had changed everything for her, and she had nothing of him left, except memories. Those memories were contained in the scorched and battered suitcase she had rescued from the fire and kept with her for all these years. It contained some old baby clothes and toys, and the only photograph she had of David. It would take a bit of reclaiming. It was in the attic, where it had been untouched for fifteen years. Just as the memories had been untouched, always there, never forgotten, just not visited. She put on some old clothes and went upstairs. A ladder had been installed in the ceiling, for easy access, but that was a fair old time ago. We'd all put on a little weight and age since then. It was a bit of a squeeze to get herself up into the loft space, but there was a helpful light. It was as dirty and undisturbed as she thought it might have been but she could see the suitcase. It wasn't as big as she remembered, but it looked substantial. 'It went up through the hatch, so it must come down again,' she said aloud to herself, and with a few grunts and expletives, and a precarious moment or two balancing it on the ladder, she managed to get it down. It was heavy. Not because of the things inside, but it was made of very sturdy, if scorched, leather banded with metal. She wiped it clean (ish) and bumped it down the stairs into the front room, putting a newspaper on the carpet first as there was still a fair chance of leaving more unnecessary marks, and she opened it up. It hadn't been locked as the keys had long been lost. It was just as she had left it, everything carefully wrapped in tissue and folded neatly inside. There was the envelope on top with 'David' written on it. She didn't want to disturb it anymore, she didn't want to rummage through and find things that she had tried to bury. She closed it again and went to find a good bungee or strap to wrap around it so that it didn't fly open on the way to Bromley. There was one of those wheeled shopping baskets under the stairs, and she wondered if the case would fit onto that. After a couple of attempts, she decided not. Not without destroying the trolley anyway.

Abigail got changed into something more presentable and called a taxi. There was no way she was taking this on the bus. She opened the front door and lifted the suitcase out onto the top step.

The taxi driver helped her load the case. He didn't have

much trouble with it, and then they set off. It was only ten minutes away and he, very kindly, unloaded it on arrival. 'You got a dead body in it, love?' he quipped. *No, but the detritus was there.*

The police station reception area was empty, save for a few chairs, and the usual posters on the walls warning about the dangers of modern life. She rested the case by the chairs and pressed the bell on the counter. A PC appeared.

'Can I help you madam?' he asked.

'Yes, I was asked to come here to meet someone. I wasn't given a name.'

'Then, what was it in connection with?' he asked noticing the suitcase. 'Is that yours Madam?'

'Oh yes, they asked me to bring anything that might help.'

'I see. Help with what, exactly?'

'There was a picture put up on television, of a man that had been stabbed, and they wanted help. Well I know who he is.'

The officer had been making notes and then he said, 'If I can take your name madam.'

She gave her details and he went back through the door. After a minute or so, a woman officer opened another door over by the side wall. 'Miss Derzel? Would you like to come this way please. I'll get someone to help with that,' pointing at the case. She called into the office and a young PC came and took the suitcase through. Abigail was directed to a small room, with two chairs and a table. She sat down.

'Would you like a cup of tea?' the officer asked.

Abigail needed something, 'Yes please. Just a little milk.' The PC nodded and left.

'Firstly, thank you for coming in. Without help from

members of the public, like yourself, our job would be considerably harder.' Abigail managed a weak smile.

'We've not had much luck in tracing any relatives in this case. How did you know this man?' She referred to the papers in front of her.

Abigail leaned forward. 'Well that's the thing you see, because he is David Lawrence. We were together, not married or anything, in 2005, and we had a little girl together. Rebecca. Rebecca went missing from the park one day when she was there with us both,' she paused, 'We looked away for just a minute.' Tears had started to sting her eyes.

The officer interrupted. 'Missing?'

'Yes, we never found her, all those years. The police couldn't find any sign of her.' Her face had started to crumple. She hadn't talked about this for so long. Just then the young PC entered the room with a cup of tea and a plate with some biscuits. 'Oh, lovely,' said the officer. 'We're really pushing the boat out, biscuits!' Abigail took a moment to recover herself.

'Thank you,' she said to the back of the young PC.

The officer continued, 'If it was reported as a missing person.'

'She,' said Abigail.

'My apologies,' said the officer and continued, 'If she was reported as a missing person, there will be a record of it. Who reported it?'

'Well, I did, with David.'

'Under what name?' she asked.

'Rebecca Derzel was her name. It would be under my name Abigail Derzel.'

'And this was in 2006, you say, can you remember the date?'

'Oh yes,' said Abigail, 'I'll never forget that day. It was the fifth of May, 2006. Friday.'

The officer wrote it down. 'Bear with me a moment will you?'

She picked up her notes and went back into the main office. Abigail looked at the case, then laid it flat on the floor and opened it up. She took out the envelope and turned it over in her hand. It wasn't sealed. She lifted the flap and took out the solitary photograph. Something she hadn't seen in so long. There they were, Abigail and David, by the car. The door open ready to leave, the picture taken from the steps of the old house. She was looking at it when the officer came back into the room. 'You haven't touched your tea,' she said.

'Er no, not yet,' Abigail replied.

'I've given the details to my colleague and he'll look it up and see what we have,' the officer said, 'Ah the suitcase, what do you have here that you think will help?'

Abigail gave her the photograph.

'Is this David with you?' she asked. 'I take it, it is you?' Abigail nodded. Then she looked a little more closely. 'We can see the registration number of the car. That will help enormously, I'll have someone put this through the computer. That will give us something, perhaps even an address to start from. What else do you have?'

Abigail pointed to the suitcase. 'That's all I have of Rebecca. I thought, maybe DNA or whatever it is you can use as clues.'

'That's very thoughtful, if the registration proves fruitless, then perhaps that may be helpful. Do you mind if we hold on to these things while we investigate?'

'I suppose, but I don't want them lost or damaged in any way, they're all I have of – '

'Of course. We will take very great care of them. Thank you very much for bringing them.' She stood up and opened the door. 'If you wouldn't mind coming along with us. Mr Lawrence is in the hospital. He is unconscious still, as far as we know, but it would be extremely helpful if you could come with us now and identify him formally for us.'

'Of course I will, but I wasn't expecting to be out for too long, I will need to get home.'

The police were very well trained, 'Don't worry madam, we have a car at our disposal. We will just drive over to the hospital and then take you straight home. It won't take long.'

At the hospital Abigail was led to a small room and a bed with the unconscious man in it. She didn't need long. 'There is no doubt. That is David. Poor man, what happened? Where was he? Who would do this?'

'All in good time madam, the investigation is ongoing. We will keep you informed and as soon as we have any news we'll be in touch. If there is anything you'd like to talk to us about in the meantime, please ring this number.' She gave her a card. 'It'll come straight through to our team.'

And that was that. The police were as good as their word and they took Abigail straight home. Being careful to drop her along the road a fair bit, so that she could be discreet. When she stepped inside the house, she didn't know quite what to do. But if ever there was a time for a glass of wine and a piece of carrot cake, this was it.

Elina stood outside the small door that said SLAS proudly on it. The door was between two shops and didn't seem to belong to either one of them. Elina turned the handle and pushed, it opened directly onto a steep staircase between two walls. The only way was up, so Elina climbed the stairs. At the top it opened out into a light and airy open plan office space, with three desks and a woman working at each one. Elina didn't know who to approach. One of the women stood up and said 'Good morning,' saving her from making that choice. 'How can we help you?'

'Hello, I am Elina Lucas. I called you last week about some information, regarding the adoption of my daughter Maeve, but you couldn't find the information.'

One of the other women, probably the senior one, looked up. 'Yes, hello. I spoke to you. It wasn't that we couldn't find the information. There just isn't any. We have checked our records to see if there's any mistake. There wasn't any adoption notice, or any reference to one in the file.'

Elina found the papers in her bag and showed them to the woman saying 'Look, here. South London Adoption Society, and further down, baby Maeve.'

She took the sheets from Elina and sat down. Elina was left standing in the middle of the office, there didn't seem to be anywhere to sit. 'I'm sorry. These papers are from this office, the heading, and address etc, but they're not the right ones. These are papers for a parent to sign when they want to put their child up for adoption. The SLAS stamp is missing too.'

'I don't understand,' said Elina, starting to feel lightheaded. 'We adopted Maeve through you and she's been living as our own daughter all this time. It's just not possible.'

The woman saw Elina was working herself up into a state, and pulled a chair out from somewhere behind her. 'Please, sit down. This isn't the document you would have. You would have a pink original which you would have signed and the corresponding white copy would be lodged in our file. There would also be a second original, also signed by you and your husband, lodged with the court, ratifying the adoption, and we would have a copy of that too. I'm afraid your daughter wasn't adopted through us. If those are the only documents you have, then she wasn't officially adopted at all. If she has been living in your household for all that time, then there will be questions that need answering. I'm afraid we're going to have to make a statement to the police.'

Elina couldn't speak. She could not understand. She couldn't think. Maeve was her world. Her daughter. She stood up, and left without a further sound. Out onto the street, the sounds hit her like a physical slap. She walked, which way, where to, didn't matter. How did this happen? What does this do to Maeve? To their small world? Who is she now? Elina could not see forward, she couldn't understand the past. Was everything a lie? If only she could speak to Devon, he would clear it all up. There would be an explanation. She got on a bus, because it was somewhere to sit down. She watched the shops going by the window, the people living their lives. It started to get dark, the nights were drawing in now. She'd better get home. She waited for the bus to stop and got off. She secured a cab, gave her address, and closed her eyes. It was stuffy but she didn't care. The cab arrived, she paid and got out. She fumbled the key into the lock and went upstairs. Maeve was in the living room; as soon as she heard the door, she jumped up spilling Rosie from her comfortable place, and ran to the top of the stairs to meet Elina coming up.

'Elina!' she cried. 'Dot's dead! She had a heart attack. I was out with Rosie and I came back, the door was wide open and she was on the floor. I called the ambulance, and when they got here. She was – dead.'

Maeve held onto Elina tightly letting the sobs come.

~

Elina didn't open the shop the next day. She barely got herself out of bed. Maeve was still full of life and had, as yet, had no reaction to her change in lifestyle. Elina managed to get break-fast ready and. drive Maeve to school, but she felt dead behind her eyes. She arrived home, parked the van as usual and went in the back way, to see two police officers standing outside the shop door peering in. She opened the door and one of them said 'Mrs Lucas?' They identified themselves.

'Yes, I'm Mrs Lucas, what can I do for you?'

'May we come in, we need to talk to you.' Elina's first thought was Maeve, but that wasn't possible. She'd just dropped her off at school and there wouldn't have been time. Dot. 'Is it about Dot? Sorry, Dorothea.'

The second officer, a smaller woman, said 'No. Is there somewhere we can sit down?'

'Of course. Follow me. I'm sorry I haven't had time to tidy up. I've just dropped my – my daughter off at school. Would you like a cup of tea?' She was talking, so that they wouldn't. She didn't want to know if anything else was about to hit her. Inevitably the first officer said 'Could you tell us if you know anyone by the name Devon Lucas, or David Lawrence?'

'Lawrence no, but Devon Lucas, yes, he's my – he was my husband.' *What was going on?*

'Is this him?' asked the officer producing a photograph from a folder that Elina hadn't noticed. She looked at the picture. He was older, tired and unshaven, even shabby looking. He always used to be so smart, so handsome. She nodded. 'Yes,' she said 'That's him.'

The second officer spoke, 'We are sorry to have to tell you, but there was an incident a short while ago, in which he was the victim of an attack. Unfortunately he hasn't yet recovered consciousness.'

Elina took a sharp intake of breath. She suddenly felt over-whelmed, like she had at the SLAS, but after so long? 'What happened? Where is he?' she asked. 'How did you come to be here?'

'Some information has come into our possession with your name on it. You were married at one time? There are no other relatives that we can find. The incident took place not far from here in fact, but we need to ask you to come to the hospital with us to confirm his identity, if you could manage it.' Elina didn't react. 'When you feel ready of course. Here is the number to call. Could you make it as soon as possible please, so that we can proceed with the investigation without any unnecessary delay?'

Elina still said nothing but as the two police officers got up to leave, she decided. 'No. I want to see him. I want to see him now.' On the way out Elina picked up the post which had fallen to the floor from the letterbox, and put it in her bag.

Maeve had been dropped off at the usual time, the usual place, and had got out of the van. Elina had been quiet. Why was Elina not as excited as Maeve was? She could hardly contain herself, but she had no-one to talk to about it. No-one at school at least.

She could have spoken to Elliot, he would have understood – or would he? Was he just like everyone else? There to make fun, to take advantage? Because he did take advantage, big time. She had opened up to him, trusted him, dropped her guard. Well, never again. She saw the clones across the road. They had held back from going in the gates, and they were watching her. They pretended to be chatting amongst themselves as everyone walked past them but, from the sly glances and the sniggers that they didn't even bother hiding, she knew what was going to happen. She knew them too well. This wouldn't be the first time. It was the first time, however, that she had felt like this about herself. She crossed the road and as expected they moved along and blocked the gate. Jane Pedersen was taller than Maeve. She stepped forward, with that sneer on her lips. Always that sneer. The other two nudging each other and waiting, anticipating. Jane tilted her head to one side. Maeve slammed her fist into Jane's face! Square on her nose. Blood flew out immediately, and Jane hit the floor sitting, shocked, with both hands covering her face. The other two screamed and everyone turned round. Maeve carried on walking into school, as if nothing had happened.

She went to her desk and picked the things that she wanted to take home. She waited. It wasn't long before she heard the sobbing, running along the corridor past the classroom. Then the tap, tap, tap of heels coming back, with the sobbing continuing behind. 'There she is!' they cried, almost in unison. The headmistress silenced them.

'Would you come into my office and explain yourself, Miss Lucas?' It wasn't a question.

'No,' said Maeve quietly, 'I don't think I will, Miss Richards. I think I shall go home. Thank you.'

The clones, who's expressions were of the 'You're going to get it' kind, suddenly stood open mouthed as Maeve walked past them and out of the building.

'Miss Lucas – Miss Maeve Lucas! I'm warning you!' came from behind her, but she took no notice. The world had changed for Maeve; now she had potential and she wasn't going to take shit from anyone. She walked home. It took a while and, although it was cold, her pace and her mood kept her warm. The look on Jane's face would keep her smiling for years.

The shop was closed and she didn't have a key to get in, but there was a master lock key safe by the back door. She wouldn't make Elina come down. She bent down and put in the code, retrieved the key, and let herself in. Straight away she heard Rosie's paws scampering on the hall floor and then she almost tumbled down the stairs in her hurry to greet Maeve. After a mass of cuddles and kisses and wags and woofs, Maeve managed to get to the stairs. No Elina to see what was going on. She called, 'Elina!' There was no answer. She threw her bag onto her bed as she passed the bedroom door and carried on into the living room. No. She could see there was no-one in the kitchen. Elina must have gone out.

The corridor was quite stark. Elina pulled her coat tighter. The young doctor checked the document in his hand and pulled the door open for her to enter. There was only one bed inside and she could barely see the occupant through the tangle of tubes and cables surrounding him. It was a formality. Of course it was Devon. The years had changed him, but not unrecognisably.

Elina nodded. 'Oh my Days! It is Devon. He looks so tired. How did he come to this?'

'Thank you,' said the officer. 'Would you come with us back to the police station, there are one or two things we need to clear up.'

'Now?' asked Elina. 'It's been such a long time since I've seen him. Poor baby.' She touched his cheek. The officer looked at the doctor, who nodded.

'There is nothing you can do here for now or the foreseeable future I'm afraid.'

'If you wouldn't mind madam,' said the officer, indicating the door. It all sounded very formal and serious.

At the station, Elina was shown into the interview room, and followed in by the officer. 'Thank you for your help with identifying Mr Lucas, we know these things are often difficult,' she said. 'There was a question brought up about your ex-husbands identity.'

'Really?' Elina was surprised.

'Yes,' said the officer, 'You see, he has already been identified by another person as a Mr David Lawrence. We checked the registration of a car, that we were told belonged to him, and it came up with your address and Mr Devon Lucas as being the last known keeper. That's why we need to speak with you.'

'That's not possible,' said Elina, matter of factly, 'I've just looked at him. There's no question. He was my husband. I've never even heard of a David Lawrence.'

The officer placed the photograph of Abigail and Devon on the table. Elina looked at it and confirmed, 'Yes, that's him. Wait – that woman, I've seen her before.'

The police officer looked up. Elina looked in her bag and

brought out the three photographs. 'There!' she said, 'I'm sure that's her, and that's Devon again with my daughter.'

The officer picked up the photographs and compared them. 'It certainly looks like the same person.' She asked, 'When were these photographs taken?'

'I have no idea, I only saw them for the first time the other day; it was an undeveloped film in the back of a drawer, but looking at Maeve, she could only have been a few months old here, so that would make it 2006 and it would have to be before October, because that's when she came to us.'

The officer wrote down the dates. 'Came to you, what do you mean?'

'She's adopted, you see we couldn't have children.'

'Do you have the adoption papers at home, just to confirm the dates?'

'No, I've got them here. They're still in my bag. And her birth certificate.'

She pulled the papers out of the bag and gave them to the officer. After a cursory glance, the officer said, 'This birth certificate names a Mr David Lawrence as the father. I thought you said you'd never heard of him?'

'Really?' said Elina. It was her turn to be surprised. 'It's odd, I went to the adoption society to see if this woman was her natural mother, but they said those papers weren't even real! I don't know what's going on.'

'We have spoken to the woman in the picture, and she says that her daughter was kidnapped in 2006. Would you know anything about that?'

'No, of course not. What are you saying?'

'I'm saying that we need to investigate these details further. Do you have any ID documents on you? Driver's licence for example?' said the officer. 'And as we are here, we will need to check on your daughter too. Could she come into the station so we can do an ID test for her? It's very simple, just a cotton bud to obtain a little DNA.'

'I think you already have her DNA, that is if you've been doing your jobs properly.' Elina was getting cross, nervous, and feeling suddenly under suspicion. '*My* daughter has been raped very recently and you have all our identities and fluids and whatever else it was you took. What's happening with all that? We all know who it was.'

'Raped?' That surprised the officer, and she was unsure for a second. 'What is your daughter's name again?'

'I've told you and you wrote it down there,' she pointed an accusing finger at the notepad. 'It's Maeve Lucas. M.A.E.V.E. L.U.C.A.S.'

'One moment,' said the officer and left the room.

Elina was left on her own, wondering what on earth was going on. To give herself something to occupy her hands for a moment, she took the morning post out of her bag. There were only two letters and both looked official, 'Bills, no doubt,' she murmured. She opened the first one. It was from the lab with the results of Maeve's blood test. She scanned it quickly for the familiar numbers. Odd. The results were all clear, and not just clear as in 'and within normal parameters', but perfect. Not a decimal point off. She checked the name on the form, perhaps it was a mix up. Maeve Lucas. 'My God!' she exclaimed aloud, just as the officer came back in the room. 'It *is* a miracle. It's a bloody miracle. Thank the Lord. Oh my God!'

'I'm sorry?' the officer said, 'What's happened?'

'It's my daughter, the blood test. She's cured.'

'I see, well, frankly, I'm embarrassed. We do have the records, as you say, from the attack.'

'The rape!'

'Yes, the alleged rape of course, and we will run the tests. Thank you for your time. That's all we need you for just now, but we may very well be in touch for further information. We'll hold on to these documents for checking if you don't mind. Can we find you at this address that you've given us?'

'Yes,' said Elina. She quickly picked up her bag and left, her only thought. 'She's been healed by God through the pastor, Praise the Lord!'

She knew where the pastor lived. She caught the bus, and hugged herself all the way home. Maeve was in, that was a surprise. She quickly went inside and nearly crushed her in a tight, tight clinch. 'What are you doing home at this time? Never mind you can tell me later.' She kissed her cheek and near to tears, told her the news. 'Here it is,' she said, 'In black and white.' She laughed, 'You're clear of it. It's a miracle. The pastor was right.' She picked up the van keys and went straight out again. Maeve hadn't said a word.

She couldn't wait. A miracle like this needs to be broadcast to the world. People have to know. She knew that she had discovered, that after years of doubt and half belief, that God was in his heaven, there was no doubt now. She had to tell the pastor. God must have been watching that journey, the way she was driving, because she arrived safely. She leapt out of the van, didn't bother to lock it and ran to the door of the house. She hammered on the door. After an eternity, the door opened. He was there. Elina fell to her knees 'Thank you father, you have saved her. Your faith has cured her. Maeve is free to live her life.

Praise the Lord. Pray with me, Father.' She took his hand and kissed it over and over, she bent her head for prayer.

'My child,' said Ben. 'Please, stand up, come inside.' Looking to see if anyone had observed them. 'Come, come.' He led her into the kitchen where Abigail was loading the dishwasher. She looked up as they came in and Ben sat Elina down at the table, her back to Abigail. Elina hadn't taken her eyes from the pastor the whole time, and meekly allowed herself to be led in.

'Elina, your daughter, we are so sorry. Elliot's upstairs. He is so upset.'

'No! That's not it. Upset. Him? I don't care.' Elina insisted, 'You cured her. She has lived with this condition, and it's incurable, well it was, and you came to our shop that night. I didn't know, how could I, that God was leading you to us, and you, you cured her.'

'Oh, my dear woman,' said Ben.

'I'll leave you to it shall I?' said Abigail, closing the door of the machine. Elina noticed her for the first time.

'Thank you, thank you.' She stopped, 'I've seen you. You're her.' Abigail was a little taken aback.

'Her, who?' she asked.

'The woman with my husband!'

'I beg your pardon!' said a shocked Abigail, 'Your husband?'

'Yes. In the picture.' Again she pulled the pictures out of her bag, spilling some of the other contents onto the floor. Ben bent to pick it up, Elina ignored him now, 'There in the picture, look!'

Abigail took the picture. 'It's David, with Rebecca. David wasn't your husband.'

'Yes he was, I mean he wasn't David or anything. His name is

Devon. Devon Lucas. I don't know who Rebecca is, but he's there with our daughter Maeve.'

'Where did you get this? That's my daughter Rebecca, that was kidnapped. Do you think I don't know my own daughter? Even after all this time. I don't know where you got that photograph, but I was the one that took it. I was standing there with them. It was the last time I ever saw my beautiful daughter.'

'That is Maeve, she has been my daughter since she was adopt – ed sixteen years ago.' Elina knew. It suddenly made sense. Devon. *He had taken the baby.* 'Is, was Devon, David, the father?'

Abigail sunk to her knees, she was crying. 'Yes.' *Is it possible, could it be possible, that after all this time, she had found Rebecca, that she was alive and nearby.* Ben watched, he wasn't sure quite what was happening. Abigail suddenly lifted her head and looked at Ben, 'Rebecca is the girl that Elliot is accused of assaulting.'

'RAPING!' shouted Elina, 'Can nobody say the word? She was raped.' She turned to Ben. 'By your son!' back to Abigail, 'And her name is Maeve!'

Like a cornered animal she searched for a way out. She didn't want to be here any more. She pushed the chair away and ran for the door, then outside and into the van. She locked the doors from inside, barricading herself in. Then looked for her keys to start it up. They'd fallen on the floor in the kitchen. There was a tap on the window. Ben stood there holding the keys out to her. She wound the window down far enough to take them from him and, crying, drove home, very much slower than she had when she had arrived.

Back in the house, Abigail had picked up the phone and called the police on the private number she'd been given. 'I know who kidnapped my daughter and I want you to get her back.'

Elliot crept back upstairs from his position behind the door. He could hardly believe what he'd heard. Maeve was Abigail's daughter. That would make them cousins.

'FUUUUUUCK!' the inside of his head exploded.

THE BOOK OF CONSEQUENCE

*T*he phone call came to Abigail first. It was the moment she had been waiting sixteen years for. Rebecca had been found! The DNA from a hair found on the baby blanket that Abigail had kept all that time had proved an exact match with that of Maeve Lucas. The police wanted to keep hold of the suitcase and its contents though to help with another ongoing investigation, regarding the identity of Devon Lucas – aka David Lawrence – and they said that they may need to speak with Abigail further. She wanted to go now. She wanted to find her Rebecca, to bring her home, to give her all the love she had kept burning inside her these years gone by. She wanted to but she knew she daren't. Rebecca wouldn't even know her. Too much too soon would frighten her away, and that was the last thing Abigail wanted. She would have to wait for the law to take its course. In the meantime she could clean. One day soon, Rebecca will come back to her and she wanted to make her home a place of welcome, a place to be proud of, so she began. Every little corner, every piece of furniture, behind the pictures on the walls, she would clean it all. She would be thorough. Maybe she should redecorate, but wait, no, she'd share that, use that to bond with Rebecca when she came. The spare bedroom would be perfect for her, and her mind was spinning with ideas for new furniture, colour schemes, and curtains. She went upstairs to tell Elliot that he'd better start tidying and cleaning his space ready. *Elliot. How was he going to cope with this?* 'We'll deal with that as and when it arises,' she said to herself. As she got to the top of the stairs, she was surprised to find his door open.

'Elliot?' she called pushing the door. No response. She went inside. It was in its normal state, clothes on the floor, spare parts for his bicycle decorating the windowsill, and bits of this and that project everywhere. On the big wall opposite the bed was a huge map of London with route lines drawn in highlighter and coloured pins at, what seemed to her, random places. The bed wasn't made, surprise, surprise, so Abigail started there.

She stripped the bed, and wondered how long it had been since Elliot had changed his sheets, there were old tissues under the pillow, she didn't remember him having a cold, and screwed up pyjamas stuffed down the side of the mattress. Abigail took the dirties downstairs. That washing machine is going to come under serious pressure over the next few days. She opened the small cupboard under the sink and donned a pair of yellow rubber gloves, and picked up the cleaning products that she needed. She took a deep breath.

~

Elliot was on his bike wearing his distinctive bright yellow helmet, cycling as fast as the roads and traffic would allow across town to where Maeve's shop was. He had to tell her.

The cold air on his face made him feel alive. It encouraged him. On his bike, Elliot felt like a superhero, flying along, avoiding dangers, darting between the monster lorries and buses, and down narrow lanes to achieve his goal. There it was. It was closed. It said so on the door, but he could see movement inside at the back. He leant his bike against the wall, locking it this time, and knocked on the door. Nothing happened. He banged louder. This time he saw someone moving about and coming to see. It was Maeve's mother. She gestured to go away. Elliot needed to speak to Maeve. He banged the door again. This time there was a little dog yapping around her heels and somebody coming from the stairs at the side.

'Maeve!' he shouted, 'Maeve I need to talk to you.'

Maeve turned to go back upstairs.

'I'm sorry,' Elliot shouted. 'I didn't mean to hurt you. I didn't understand. Please forgive me. Maeve.' The shouting had turned to pleading. Maeve stopped. Her mother said something to her. Maeve looked at the door, shrugged, and stood behind her mother, looking at Elliot. Elina unlocked the door and opened it a little. Elliot moved to go in but Elina held it firm.

'What are you doing here?' she spat.

'I need to tell you, I would never hurt Maeve. I love her!' He was almost crying. Elina looked at him and snorted a laugh.

'Fuck off Elliot. Don't ever come anywhere near us again.'

'But I cured her! The pastor gave it to her after. But it was when we – were together, I cured her. Not him!'

Rosie continued yapping, as if echoing Elina's sentiments. Elina closed the door and walked back into the shop. He shouted again, reaching for the last straw, 'We're related. We're cousins. Maeve!'

She just stood there looking at him. The dog was still barking. She picked it up and it quietened; then she turned and disappeared upstairs. He stood there for a minute. *But I loved her and I'd told her. Isn't that what you were supposed to do?*

He didn't understand. They had been together, she'd run away afterwards. He'd gone about it all wrong and it had turned into something it wasn't meant to be. He'd made a mistake. *Why won't she talk to me? Then I could make her understand.*

Elliot got back on his bike. He was upset so much that he'd forgotten it was locked. He leant down and turned the little dial. It snapped open. He reached and freed the chain from the wheel, left the chain there, and cycled away. He needed somewhere to think, to sort this out in his mind. It wasn't on purpose, how could anyone possibly think that. Now she hated him. He kept his head down. Now the cold was biting, the traffic choking, and the lorries terrifying. His mind racing, on and on he went. Before he realised it he had crossed over the river and was heading north, back on the familiar route that he'd ridden so many times. The bike leading the way. It had taken forever but felt like no time at all. Freezywater ahead, on the right the reservoir. He turned along Nag's Head road and stopped at the water's edge, or as near as he could get. He sat down.

It was the blood. This legacy his father had told him about. He didn't want any part of his father, or the church, or the centre, or this curse that had been at the root of all his problems. There was a small toolkit attached to the back of the saddle, it was velcro'd shut. He ripped it open and took out the small knife he kept there. He thought of the things he would lose. Only Maeve, and his bike. He cut quickly and deep into his wrist and watched the thick red liquid well up and flow out of his vein and pour into a widening circle, vivid against the fresh green of the grass.

It didn't take long for the police to get back in touch with Elina. They didn't phone, they called at the shop again. 'We need you to come back to the station with us, if you wouldn't mind,' they said, 'There have been one or two things that have come up, that just need clearing up.' Elina was more concerned about Maeve and Rosie being left in the house. 'Is there a neighbour that could come in for a while to sit with them?' the police constable said.

'No, I don't think so.'

'It shouldn't be for too long. How old is your daughter?'

'Sixteen,' said Elina.

'Oh, she will be fine,' the police officer said, 'But if you are at all concerned, we can arrange for someone from social services to come and sit with her.'

'No, no. I think it will be alright. I'll be back for her tea I expect?' asked Elina hopefully.

'I can't say madam, we have only been asked to come and drive you.'

'Could you come in for a moment, while I get my coat and tell Maeve what's happening?' She let them in and went up to the flat. They waited in the shop, looking at the flowers. A moment or two later Elina reappeared.

'These are lovely,' said the WPC, pointing at some potted plants near to the door.

'Aren't they though?' commented Elina, 'They're actually a very common flowering plant. Don't tell everybody but they just grow everywhere. *Nerium Oleander* is their name, Pliny the elder even referred to them one time. Aren't they lovely?'

The WPC leaned over to smell the flower. 'Lovely,' she echoed.

They got into the waiting police car, and drove to the station. Elina was taken into the same room as before. She thought it was the same room, unless they had identical ones. She sat down. She was joined by the same female police officer as before.

'Thank you again for coming in like this. I'm sorry to have to tell you, there have been some problems.'

'Oh,' said Elina. In truth, she didn't know what to say.

'Yes.' The police officer went on. 'The adoption documents, as you were told I understand, are not official documents at all; they have been adapted by a Mr Anthony Joshua, as it's his name that's mentioned, to hide the disappearance of the child. The birth certificate is also a copy that has been altered. It is very difficult to tell at the moment but the father, the man you know as Devon Lucas, has put the name David Lawrence in place of his own and the child's name has been changed to Maeve after copying. We shall know for certain soon, but I'm willing to bet that the name underneath is Rebecca. Will we find that the change is in your handwriting? We have already established that Mr Lucas and Mr Lawrence are the same person. Do you have anything to add, that may enlighten us further?'

'No!' Elina was getting upset, 'Devon said she was called Maeve, and I liked it so we kept it.'

'It was your husband's idea?'

'Yes. No. I don't know.'

'Were you so desperate for a child, that you and your husband planned and carried out the abduction of the child known as Rebecca Derzel?'

Elina was panicking now. 'I've never heard of Rebecca Derzel, or David Lawrence for that matter. I don't know any of them.'

'The name David Lawrence was on that birth certificate, in your possession for sixteen years, and you say that in all that time, you never once read it?'

'No, I er – No, I don't...' stammered Elina.

'And the marriage certificate is signed by Mr Anthony Drew Joshua?' She produced the document from a folder on the table.

'Who?' said Elina.

'He is well known to us, but more commonly as Adey Joshua. Does that ring a bell? It is his name on the adoption papers and he is a man very well known to us, with a very long record. What can you tell us about that association?'

'He was our best man.'

'Owing to these anomalies coming to light, we investigated a little further into Mr Lucas, and we've not been able to find any records of him before your marriage. Unfortunately the documents presented for obtaining the licence for that were counterfeit, again involving Mr Joshua, which, I'm sorry to say throws the legality of your marriage and your husband's, sorry ex husband's, residency in this country into doubt. The camera containing the photographs was by your own admission, in your possession. Do you have the camera still?'

'No, the photo place kept it, it was a throwaway camera from years ago. They only gave me the pictures.' Elina was getting desperate.

'Then if you would write down the name of the shop concerned, we will check with them.' She gave Elina a pen and a piece of paper, which was then passed into the folder beside her.

'Due to the gravity of the offence of abduction, Mrs Lucas, and the amount of evidence, albeit some of it is circumstantial, that we have that links you and your husband to these events; we have no choice but to caution you and to place you under arrest under the child abduction act of 1984 for the abduction of Rebecca Derzel. You do not have to say anything. But, it may harm your defence if you do not mention when questioned something which you later rely on in court. Anything you do say may be given in evidence. Do you understand?'

'Yes,' said Elina, starting to panic. 'What about Maeve? Who'll look after her?'

'Don't worry, we'll have social services send someone to look after her and get her sorted for the night. It's a pity we can't speak to Mr Lucas just yet, but as soon as we are able to we will be needing a statement from him as well.'

A passer by found him. She noticed his yellow helmet first. She thought it was odd, the young man sitting there in the cold when she went past with her dog, and he was still there, still wearing the yellow helmet, when she came back, even though it was starting to get dark. She had called out to him, and finally gone over there, but as she had approached him she had seen the large dark stain in front of him and called the police.

The police went to the Pastor's house. He opened the door

himself 'Not again. Haven't we had enough of police in the last few days?' he said.

'We're sorry sir, but are you Mr Ben Saphan?' the officer said.

'Yes, I am,' he said impatiently.

'May we come inside, we need to talk to you for a moment.'

'If it's about Elliot, we are very aware of what he's done.'

'Oh, you know already sir. I'm sorry, we've only just heard ourselves. In that case, we need to ask you if you would come to the mortuary at your earliest – '

'The mortuary? Why?'

'To identify your son sir.'

'But he's not dead!'

'Sir, you said you knew.'

Ben's eyes rolled up, his whole body swayed and toppled like a great tree, and he hit the ground flat. He rolled halfway down the steps, knocking one of the officers over and unbalancing the other. Abigail, in her apron and rubber gloves came from the kitchen to see what was happening, and screamed. An ambulance was called immediately after the officers had recovered their feet. Abigail was sat down and given a drink of water. It was an unusually difficult situation for the police to deal with, but they managed, sensitively, to tell Abigail the reason for their visit and the probable cause of Ben's collapse. The tears welled up 'Ben, I told you. I told you he needed help.' Then, more wistful than anything, and finding it hard to speak, 'That's it then. The end,' she said, 'Oh, Hannah.'

'Beg your pardon madam?' said the officer sitting with her.

'Oh nothing, nothing at all.'

The ambulance with the paramedics arrived and tended to Ben. When they were satisfied that he was comfortable, they helped Abigail into the ambulance with him and closed the doors. The police officers were left on their own as they heard the siren disappearing into the distance. They went round the house switching off the lights and checking the doors. They found a key they could give to Abigail if she had gone without one and put it in an evidence bag. It was all they had. They closed the door and left.

These things take a long time to arrange, especially if the police have got any cases connected to the deceased. In this case, there was the rape allegation. In death Elliot could no longer be prosecuted, although the case had been recorded as a criminal act with the perpetrator deceased.

There was Abigail, his Aunt and protector, crying not just for Elliot, but for what had been lost. Maeve was there. She was now known to be his cousin and she was present with a social worker from the Greenwich Children's home, where she had been looked after ever since Elina had been arrested. She was curious. There was no doubt that Abigail was her mother. DNA tests had proved that beyond a doubt. That was why the social worker was there. To forestall any inappropriate contact. Abigail hadn't been permitted to meet with Maeve, until Maeve decided whether she wanted to. She'd seen pictures but that wasn't the same thing. She had looked forward to the funeral. She needed some comfort, someone warm and safe to hold but there was no-one. Her thoughts turned to Rosie who, much to Maeve's horror and heartbreak, was being kept in kennels away from her at least until Elina's case was determined. Elina had pled not guilty and the case was due to be heard in the crown court at some point, undetermined as yet, in the future.

Abigail's time, these days, was taken up looking after Ben. When he had collapsed he was rushed to hospital in time to save his life, although a lot of his functionality had gone. It had been cut away in one swift stroke. They kept him at the hospital until Abigail, and the church, could organise the house into a suitable place to care for him. They had insisted on a care package being put in place with a regime of carers, an appropriate bed with all the necessary safety features, a bathroom fitted with all the aids needed, and a myriad of other things; not the least of which was cupboard space to hold all the medicines, and pads, and creams that needed to be applied regularly. So far though a suitable package hadn't been found.

When Dot had died, she had left a substantial amount in trust for Maeve and Elina, with a solicitor appointed as trustee to administer it until Maeve's eighteenth birthday. It was enough that Maeve would be able to be independent for a fair while whilst she decided what path her life would take.

The vicar started the short service. There was a pre-recorded hymn, Dvorak's symphony number 9, 'Going Home', a short prayer and the 'Ashes to ashes, dust to dust' thing, and it was over. Piped music played loudly to cover the noise of the motor taking the coffin away while they waited. Outside, against the wall were two wreaths, both small. One was from Abigail and the other in the shape of a bicycle from the online WhatsApp group of his friends. Maeve stopped by them and Abigail brushed past her, probably on purpose, and as she did so, she smiled at Maeve. There was a tear in her eye, and she was gone. The social worker took Maeve back to Abbey Wood.

~

Six weeks later Elina was brought to trial. She was found guilty. Her lawyer wasn't a top city lawyer, he was employed by the state to help people who can't afford top city lawyers. He didn't seem to make much of an argument. Perhaps he thought Elina was guilty from the start. The jury didn't believe her. She broke down, protested her innocence, but to deaf ears. She was taken down to the cells to await sentencing. Her lawyer said that they were very definitely going to open an appeal, but she didn't have money or connections, or a forceful personality. She believed the odds were not good. What she did think though, and it consoled her, was that it was a fair price to pay. God had saved her daughter and Maeve was her daughter, no matter what anybody said. She had loved her and loved her and loved her for sixteen years, she'd held her when she'd cried, soothed her when she was sick, fed her when there was nothing to eat. Laughed with her, and made sacrifices for her. God had given her the greatest gift. Now God wanted payment. He wanted balance.

~

Abigail wrote to Maeve at the home and, when Maeve heard about how Elina and Devon came to be her parents, she didn't know what to believe. She did know that if she stayed at the home, she would likely never get to see Rosie again. She wrote back and agreed that as long as she could have Rosie come back to her, then she would go and stay with Abigail. At least until her eighteenth birthday, which was only just over a year away. Abigail got the spare room ready. She couldn't bear to use

Elliot's room. Not yet. It was all still too raw. The court rubber stamped all the paperwork, and the taxi arrived. It sat there now, outside the main front door. Maeve wasn't sad to be leaving, she'd not been there long enough to make friends, so nothing lost. In the meantime Abigail went to the kennels to collect Rosie. Surprisingly, there was quite a bill to pay for her stay there, but no price was too high for what Abigail was gaining. Rosie was quiet, not the bouncy ball of fluff she used to be, she couldn't understand what had happened to her. *What had she done wrong?* She was in a carrying crate when Abigail arrived and took her to her new home.

Maeve didn't have much. The flower shop had closed and the landlords had gone in and cleared everything out ready to re-let it. All of Elina's things had been put in storage.

The taxi pulled up outside the house. Abigail had been watching from an upstairs window and had seen it coming down the lane. She wasn't the only one watching, someone stepped back into the shadows as the taxi arrived. She'd only just had time to get to the door with Rosie in her arms to greet Maeve. She wanted to make the best impression. The driver got out and went to the passenger side to collect Maeve's suitcase, and Maeve stood on the pavement looking around at her new surroundings. She saw no-one except the woman, Abigail, in the doorway, unable to contain a wriggling, wagging, crying Rosie for one second after she had spotted Maeve. Rosie bounded down the steps and leapt as high as she could as Maeve bent to catch her. She could hardly see her way back up the steps for Rosie licking her face.

'Welcome home, Maeve,' said Abigail. 'I do hope you will think of it as your home. I've tried to bring some of your –

some of Elina's favourite things from the shop, and your things, from your list of course, will be here soon from storage.'

She showed Maeve through the hallway, where some of the familiar plants of her childhood were now placed, and into the kitchen. The conversion of the front room to eventually accommodate Ben had already begun.

'Rosie is so pleased to see you.' Abigail smiled at her daughter. It would be hard to remember that she wasn't Rebecca, the baby she'd lost, but a young adult in her own right, with her own life and desires.

Life in this house would be very different. Elliot, the final link, gone. After his death, Maeve and Rosie would bring some of the life back.

'I am so happy that you're here Maeve, and I promise you we are going to have a wonderful future together.'

'Until I'm eighteen,' Maeve said.

'Yes, of course, until you're eighteen, but after that, who knows what the future may bring. Ben, the pastor, will come home again, we hope, although he'll never be that again, but he will keep us all busy. I mean, both busy.'

'Mrs Derzel,' said Maeve, 'Will that be my name now? Derzel.'

'Abi, please, call me Abi, and not if you don't want it to be,' Abigail reassured her.

'I just feel that I don't want to betray my mother, Elina. She's the only mum I have, I mean that I've known.' Tears started to appear but she controlled them. 'I'm sorry about what happened, with Elliot. I'm sure he didn't mean – what happened.'

Abigail took Maeve's shoulders in her hands, looked her in the eye and knowing the gift that had been lost, said, 'I know.

It's all over now though. We must have a new beginning. What about a nice cup of tea?'

'Lovely, but I need somewhere for Rosie's bowl and lead, so that she knows where she's supposed to be, and her bed needs to be with me.'

'Oh, how silly of me,' laughed Abigail, 'I haven't shown you your room or anything. Look, come on both of you I'll show you now, while the kettle boils.' She beckoned to Maeve to follow.

'Oh no,' said Maeve suddenly, 'That can't be there!' She pointed to one of the plants in the hallway, 'It's oleander, it's very toxic. If Rosie started nibbling at it, it could really hurt her.'

'Really? It was one of the plants from the shop, and it had a very nice pot, I thought you'd like it,' said Abigail, 'I'll put it somewhere else then, a bit safer and out of her way. Up the stairs and on the left. That's yours.'

Maeve went ahead and into the room. It was beautiful. There were some of her things already there. The bed had a delicately patterned lilac duvet, which looked very fluffy and cosy. The walls were a soft shade of barely pink, and there were cupboards and space to spare.

'You can arrange things how you like,' said Abigail encouragingly, 'And if you don't like the colours we can try again with something else.'

'No, it's lovely, thank you so much. You should have seen my room at Abbey Wood, more like a proper Abbey if you ask me, anything would be better than that. No, I don't mean... No. This is beautiful. Rosie look where we're going to be. We'll put your bed over there and we'll be together for always.'

The little dog was running in circles sniffing the new home

and trying to wag her tail and jump up at Maeve all at the same time. She was so excited. 'Oh, the kettle!' Maeve suddenly remembered.

'Don't worry, it'll switch itself off,' replied Abigail. 'Not like Rosie! Come along let's get that cup of tea, I must admit I am desperate.'

Abigail made the tea, in a proper teapot and on a tray with a matching milk jug, china cups, and a sugar bowl, accompanied by a plate of hobnobs.

'My goodness, I didn't know the king was coming to tea!' Maeve exclaimed.

Abigail laughed, 'Don't expect this every time, it's just that it's such a special occasion and I really wanted to make a good impression.'

'Don't worry, I'm impressed.'

'And there's a little something in Rosie's bowl too,' said Abigail, pointing at the little dog snuffling at some doggy treats, 'But I see she's found them already.' They laughed together. Abigail had dreamt, prayed, and cried so many times hoping to share a moment like this with her daughter and, as she looked over the teapot at Maeve, she couldn't help the tears filling her eyes. She quickly reached for a piece of kitchen towel, but not so quickly that Maeve didn't see. Rosie, of course, noticed nothing except the one remaining biscuit that she was chasing around her bowl with her nose.

It's often difficult getting used to new surroundings, and that night it took Maeve a while to fall asleep, not least because Rosie wouldn't – couldn't – settle either. There was so much she wanted to know. She couldn't believe all the things they said her mother, Elina, had done and what about her father, had he been nearby all this time? Had it all been lies? She determined to bring the matter up first thing in the morning with Abigail. Finally she succumbed to the warmth of the duvet and the rhythm of the little beating heart snuggled beside her.

~

'No, I only had one sister, and some cousins but they live a long way away, up in Yorkshire.' Abigail answered Maeve's question. 'And Hannah died some years ago now. So really, there is just me.'

'But what about my father, what happened to him, and why is he in the hospital now?' Maeve persisted.

'I don't know. He went away. I never heard from him afterwards, until recently. They said he was attacked with a knife, but I don't know any more than that. Whether it was a random attack, or a fight, or even an accident. All I know is that he is in a coma and although they're all hoping for the best, nobody is holding out much hope,' said Abigail.

'There's always hope,' Maeve went on, 'I was – I had a condition that everyone said was incurable, but then there was a miracle.' Rosie was pawing at her leg, 'I'll take you out in a minute darling,' she carried on, 'I have no idea how. The pastor came to our shop and seemed to go mad, praying and such, then he made me drink something. Then when I got up the next day I felt great and I've not had a problem since. Touch wood.' Maeve stood up and went to fetch Rosie's lead.

'The pastor was a very special person before his stroke,' Abigail explained, 'But I don't think there will be any more miracles from that direction.'

'It's strange but I don't think that's it. You see, Elliot came to the shop after and said something strange. He said that *he* had cured me, when he – when we… at the centre. He said it was in his blood somehow?'

'Elliot was a lovely person, a little naive for his age. I blame the pastor for that, but he might say almost anything if he was emotionally upset,' Abigail said sadly.

'No, he wasn't so much upset as passionate. He desperately tried to tell me but I wouldn't listen and then he went off. On his bike.'

'We loved him very much.' She paused for a moment, lost in her own thoughts, then said, more brightly, 'I want to go to the hospital to see David, you don't mind me calling him that do you? It's the only name I've known him by.'

Maeve shifted in the seat. 'No that's ok. All right Rosie!' said Maeve, as the little dog jumped up at her in anticipation.

Abigail continued. 'Would you like to come along? You don't have to stay long, and I doubt there will be any response from him.'

'I'd like that. I mean not the response thing, I mean I'd like to see him,' replied Maeve.

'All right then we'll go this afternoon. In the meantime we need to sort out something for lunch and start getting you two settled. Is there anything you don't like to eat?'

'No, I'm fairly easy nowadays. I used to have to have everything organic and fresh but it's alright now, although I do tend towards the vegetarian a bit.'

Abigail relaxed, she seemed to have been tense forever. 'I'm sure we can find something for you,' she said.

Maeve stood up. 'I do need to take Rosie out for a bit, she must be desperate.' She attached the lead to Rosie's collar.

'Don't be too long then,' Abigail said and the pair went out by the back door.

Rosie would have to get used to all the sights and smells of this new area, and so would she. As long as they were together, Maeve thought, things would turn out all right.

Being 'normal' did make life a lot less complicated and Maeve was sure she had Elliot to thank. Elliot had definitely said that her cure was not the pastor's doing, but his blood somehow cleansing her. How could that be?

There weren't many people about. There was another lady walking her dog, a man leaning on a wall smoking a cigarette, and a couple of cars passed. As they were walking they came across a nice expanse of green where Maeve could let Rosie off the lead. She kept a careful eye on her and had her little plastic bags at the ready while she watched. Her father was in hospital, unlikely to wake up, her mother, who was no longer her mother, in prison for kidnapping her and here she was living in a house with a stranger who was her real mother. It was a lot to take in, even if being raped by your cousin, and being miraculously cured, weren't counted. Who was she? Where did she fit in now? She needed to ask somebody. What was this blood business of Elliot's all about?

Time passed her by. She looked up. *Where was Rosie?* Nowhere to be seen. She couldn't be far though. Maeve walked on, looking about, becoming increasingly concerned. Rosie didn't usually run off but, this was all new to her, maybe she'd got herself turned around. Maeve began calling.

'Roooosieee!' Nothing. Time was getting on, she had to tell Abigail that lunch would have to wait. Suddenly a flurry of white burst out from behind a bush and jumped at her. 'Rosie! There you are. Come on we've got to get back.' Maeve re-attached the lead and set off back.

Abigail had lunch ready; tomato soup and a salad. Maeve

wasn't that hungry so it was fine. More importantly Rosie was tucking into a bowl full of goodness on the floor. 'I'm sorry it's not much,' Abigail apologised. 'But the fridge is stuffed so full, I thought if I opened a drawer I'd never close it again. I will need to sort it so you can have a little space for your own favourites.'

'No, I'll do it. It'll keep me busy until we go out. Unless there's anything else you want me to do?'

'Thank you. No, I'll sort it out for you later,' said Abigail, 'I'll do the pots while you see to Rosie then.'

Maeve finished her meal, put the plates by the sink, and checked Rosie's bowl. Empty and licked clean. She gave her some water and a few extra biscuits. In the meantime, Abigail opened the dishwasher door and piled everything inside. 'That's easy then!' said Maeve, 'We never had one of those.'

'Ben hated it,' Abigail told her, 'He complained that it was just a dirty dish cupboard. I find it very convenient.' She popped a capsule thing inside and shut the door. 'I need to go and freshen up,' she said, 'Put your feet up, we've got about an hour or so before we have to leave.'

Abigail left Maeve and Rosie to their own devices and went upstairs. Maeve opened the fridge drawer and emptied it out. 'There's no sense in sitting around doing nothing,' she said to herself. There actually wasn't much in the way of food inside. Most of the room was taken up by an opaque plastic box. Maeve lifted it out. There was a little catch but it flipped open easily. Inside were some tubes, mostly empty, but there were three in a line that had some red liquid in. Realisation suddenly hit Maeve. *This is blood. Elliot was talking about blood! Is this his?* The thought made her a little nauseous. *Is this what cured me?* Her mind raced. *Her father was in hospital in a coma. Would this cure him? Could it possibly?* She took one of the phials. There was a date on it that was about four weeks old. It looked alright. She slipped the sealed tube into her pocket, and put everything back as it was. She opened her mobile and looked up preserving blood. Approximately forty two days, it said. Blood could be kept, without freezing, for over a month! Who knew? Maeve sat in the kitchen with Rosie, playing and cuddling until it was time to go.

Abigail came down from the bedroom looking very tidy. Then the three of them got into the small car and headed off. After eventually finding a space to park, and leaving a window open for Rosie, Abigail led the way into the hospital. They found the ward, after being directed at the reception desk. They had to buzz to get in but, once they did, there he was. Abigail had been there once before, with the police to identify him, but it was still a shock seeing him like this, hooked up to all the machinery; even more so for Maeve, she didn't know this man whom they said was her father, and she had no real memory of him, since she was tiny the last time she'd seen him. A nurse came in and attached a bag at the top of a metal stand, then connected some tubes. She looked at Maeve and Abigail, 'Lunch,' she said smiling and left. Maeve stood and studied him. That face, wrinkled but peaceful, hair greying slightly, and so still. If it wasn't for the slight movement of his chest, one might have assumed he was already dead.

'Are you alright love?' asked Abigail.

'Yes, yes I'm fine. So this is my father?' said Maeve, almost to herself.

'He is.' Abigail sighed, 'Mr David Lawrence as I've known him, but he was someone else to you wasn't he?'

'Devon Lucas of Lucas's Lupins' flower shop,' replied Maeve.

'That was a long time ago. I don't really recognise him. I wish I could ask him about it all.'

'They say it's possible that he will come out of the coma, but not to hold out too much hope for now. He's had a hard time of it,' said Abigail. Then, almost shaking herself, carried on, 'Ben, the pastor, is in the hospital. In the stroke ward. Would you mind if I dropped in to see him as well? I mean you can come but – '

'No, I don't want to see him. I'll stay here for a minute and then wait in the car, if that's alright.'

Abigail gave her the keys and left.

Maybe it's all a fantasy, a fairy tale. It can't do any harm though, can it? Maeve felt the phial. Maybe it wouldn't even work. Before she could stop herself, she'd reached for the cap on the bag, taken out the phial, and broken the plastic top off. Then she poured the liquid into the bag. It went very pink. She replaced the top on the bag. *No-one would notice the pink bag for a while and then they'd probably change it. No harm done. We'll see.* She turned and left.

When they got home, Maeve went upstairs with Rosie while Abigail started work on the fridge. She cleared a whole drawer space, and started a shopping list. She called upstairs, 'Reb... Maeve! Is there anything you want from the shop?'

There was no reply. Abigail went up and gently knocked on the bedroom door, 'Maeve?'

There was a scuffle from inside and then the door opened. 'Sorry, I didn't hear you, I had my earphones in,' Maeve said.

'I was making a list for the shops. Is there anything special that you need?'

'No,' Maeve replied, 'Just to make sure that Rosie has enough treats to last her.'

'Oh yes,' Abigail laughed. 'That's at the top of the list.'

Abigail went back down, and Maeve heard her busying herself in the kitchen, then all went quiet. The car engine started and moved away. Rosie went downstairs, probably wanting to see if any treats had appeared in her bowl and Maeve followed her. She put the kettle on to make a cup of tea, got the milk from the fridge, and, out of curiosity, opened the fridge drawer. It was empty; the box had gone.

Maeve was up and dressed early. Sleeping in a new place took time to get used to and with all that was going on in her life, she'd had a fitful sleep. Even so Abigail was already up and doing. The kettle was on, she'd obviously heard Maeve get up. Rosie was sniffing her way around the house and as soon as she heard Maeve, she came bounding to her. 'Good morning Maeve!' called Abigail, perhaps a little too cheerily for that time, nevertheless Maeve grunted her politest reply.

'Mornin'.'

'She's been sniffing at the door for a while,' observed Abigail, 'I think she's trying to say something.'

'Oh, okay, I'll take her out,' said Maeve, reaching for the lead hanging on the back of the door. 'Won't be a minute, she's usually very good.'

'Alright, the kettle has boiled, I'll make you a cuppa. Don't let it get cold.'

Maeve and Rosie left her to it and walked off down the road to the same green area as before. Once there, Maeve undid the clip on the lead and let Rosie go. She stood on the path looking around at the trees, through which she could see the edge of the estate. There was a slight chill in the air but, for the time of year, not unusual, and she needed a cup of tea. She started back and called for Rosie to follow. She had to take a little care as the ground was slightly slippery. She looked behind her and called again. 'Oh no, not these games again,' she called, 'Come along Rosie, let's go!'

There was no sign of her. Maeve stopped to listen. She could hear the traffic from the main road in the background and distant voices but no scratching, chasing, snuffling sounds at all. She started walking back to where she had last seen the dog. Not a sign, and nobody about to ask either. For half an hour, Maeve walked up and down, looking everywhere she could and looking again, calling out constantly. She passed a couple who said they hadn't seen any dogs about this morning. Maeve began to get very stressed. This was not Rosie, she had never run off. Maeve had to get back and tell Abigail what was happening otherwise she would be worrying about her. Maeve started to run back to the house, it wasn't far. In a couple of minutes she was there. She burst in the back door. 'Abigail!'

Then she saw Rosie happily drinking from the bowl. 'What! How on earth did you get here?' she bent down to stroke her head. Then she saw cigarette man from the day before.

'Maeve,' Abigail breathed with relief. 'Thank goodness you're back. I've been quite worried. This kind gentleman found Rosie wandering about.'

He spoke. 'I thought she was on her own, I couldn't see you, or anybody, with her. So I brought her here,' he said.

'She wasn't lost though, well she was, but only....'. Maeve caught a fleeting look from Abigail. *What? What did that mean, was that even something?* 'It was probably my fault for not watching her, and she doesn't know the place, she's only been there once with me – once before that is – so she most likely lost her way.' Maeve couldn't seem to stop talking, *what was wrong?*

Abigail cut in, 'It's a funny coincidence though isn't it, that Tony here knows David.'

'Devin!' said Tony.

'Yes, and he'd like to visit him with me today.'

'Both of you. It would be nice if we all go to see him.' Tony sounded a little more insistent.

'How do you know him?' Maeve wanted to know everything about Devon.

'I know you too. The baby. I was his best man.' He laughed suddenly. 'Ironic i'nt it?'

'I'll stay here if that's okay? I'll need to see to Rosie, and we only saw him yesterday,' Maeve said.

'Bring the dog,' said Tony.

'I saw you, you were outside yesterday. Leaning against a wall! It was when I took Rosie out.'

'Well hooray for Sherlock. Come on get yourselves in the car.'

'They only let family in to see him so there's no point really.' Maeve was being somewhat naive.

'I am family now. I'm your bloody uncle Tony, get moving.'

'Maeve!' said Abigail sharply, 'Just do it.'

Rosie started to growl toward him, but kept safely behind Maeve. Maeve picked Rosie up and they were all ushered to the door. Maeve climbed into the front passenger seat and held Rosie on her lap. Tony got in the back. The small car suddenly seemed tiny. Abigail drove cautiously to the hospital. The car park was full so Tony told them, 'Stop at the side here, never mind the lines, and lead the way.'

Abigail went first followed by Maeve. 'Leave the dog in the fuckin' car,' he said glaring at Maeve, 'And you, give me the keys.'

They went into the hospital, along the corridors; Abigail hoping the room David was in would be a hive of activity. They reached the ward and pressed the buzzer. They heard the door click and they went through. Devon wasn't there!

'What the fuck's this?' fumed Tony. 'What are you trying to pull? Where is he?'

Abigail turned and marched to the nurses station. 'Mr Lucas, room 6A. Has he been moved?' she demanded.

'No. He discharged himself this morning,' said the nurse, 'The doctor needs to speak to you. She said as soon as anybody comes in asking for him.'

Abigail was stunned. 'But we were here yesterday. He was in a coma, he couldn't respond to anything, let alone get up and leave.'

Tony appeared behind her holding on to Maeve's arm. 'Something's going on here. We're leaving. Open the door!' The nurse just looked at him. 'Open the fuckin' door!'

They got to the main door and heard the click. Tony ushered them out of the hospital and back to the car. Abigail stood by the car door waiting for the keys. 'Get in the car!' he hissed at her.

'You've got the keys,' she barked back. He fumbled in his pocket and tossed them to her. They squeezed back in, Maeve taking control of Rosie. Once inside, Tony pulled a hunting knife from his inner pocket. 'Straight back,' he said quietly, regaining his composure again. Abigail drove carefully all the way. The car pulled up, they got out and went inside the house.

'I need something to eat. Get something ready for us,' he ordered, 'Don't try anything stupid. I've used this before.'

'On David, no doubt,' countered Abigail. 'Obviously you're not very good with it.'

'His name's Devon, I've known him long enough.'

'What was that you said earlier, about a baby?' Abigail wasn't sure she'd heard him properly.

'Baby? Oh, this one,' he laughed, pointing at Maeve, who was still holding a wriggling Rosie. 'You should ask your friend "David" about that. Now we're all going to sit down quietly and you're going to tell me where he is.'

'I need the toilet first,' Abigail said, walking to the door. 'Maeve, would you get some vegetable soup out of the cupboard, please?'

Abigail went out and Maeve opened the cupboard, pulled out a couple of tins of thick vegetable soup and opened them up, emptied them both into a pan, and turned on the gas. They heard the toilet flush and Abigail returned. She fetched a loaf from the basket, sliced and buttered it. 'I hope you washed your hands,' smirked Tony.

Rosie finally escaped Maeve's arms and went to attack Tony, who kicked her away before she even got to him. Tony sat down whilst Maeve got some spoons out of the drawer. Abigail meanwhile was chopping up some herbs. 'A little basil always helps any situation,' she said.

Maeve put the spoons on the table, 'You won't need a knife for the bread then, will you?' She'd learned about sarcasm at school.

Nobody spoke until the soup was ready. There was nothing to say. Maeve went to pick up the bowls that Abigail had prepared. Abigail made certain that she saw her sprinkle the herb onto one of the bowls and stir it. Then pointing at another one said, 'That one's yours!' She picked up the last one for herself. Tony was really hungry, as if he hadn't eaten for a while. He devoured the soup and bread and wanted more. Abigail obliged.

'Right, we've been having fun together. Now where is he?'

'I don't know,' said Abigail, 'I told you, I thought he was in the hospital.'

'I don't either, we saw him there yesterday, he was very bad,' added Maeve, unnecessarily as it happened.

'I know that, I've been watching, I saw you arrive.'

'Was it you? All those years ago, in the park? You're his friend Adey aren't you?' Abigail breathed. 'You're not Tony anyone.'

He laughed, 'What's a name? Yes I am. Anthony, middle name Drew. A.D. As you well know.'

'Who?' Maeve was confused.

Then they heard the noise. It came from outside. Adey froze for a second, then leapt up, grabbed Rosie with one hand, and held the knife to her. He stood behind the back door. The handle moved quietly and slowly, so as not to be noticed but they were all staring at it intently. Suddenly it burst open and Devon almost fell in. Adey immediately dropped the dog and thrust the knife at Devon, he missed and his impetus carried him forward. Devon turned, grabbed hold of him tightly and tried to catch the arm holding the knife. The two struggled against each other, Devon less fit than his opponent, and still bandaged where he had been attacked previously. Suddenly Adey bent double and groaned. He let go and fell. Devon stepped back and picked up the knife that had been dropped onto the kitchen floor. He knelt towards the stricken figure.

'No!' said Abigail, who had backed away and was standing beside Maeve, offering a little protection. 'Just wait!'

'What's happening?' Maeve cried.

'It wasn't basil,' said Abigail. 'When you chop herbs they look pretty much the same.'

'What was it?' Maeve and Devon almost asked together.

'You know what it was,' Abigail looked at Maeve. 'You told me to move it in case Rosie nibbled at it.'

'The Oleander?'

'Oleander, but that's – of course it is.' Devon hadn't worked with Elina and learned nothing about plants. 'We can't leave him there.'

'We need to get him to the hospital quickly,' said Maeve.

'We're doing nothing of the sort!' Abigail stood up and looked at the figure writhing on the floor.

'Or get the blood that was in the fridge,' Maeve blurted out.

'I knew there were three,' said Abigail. 'David, whatever has gone on. Now you can clean the slate. You will take the blame for this. Take him in the big car, in the garage, dump him somewhere he won't be found.' Devon nodded.

'But he's not dead!' Maeve insisted.

Abigail was calm, 'Not yet, but he will be soon. Look at the oleander, there's not much of it left.' She was at peace with herself as she felt that justice was served.

'I can't lift him on my own,' said Devon, 'This wound hasn't healed properly yet.'

'I'll help, Maeve get those keys, on the hook there,' she pointed, 'And open the garage door. Don't worry about the wound David, it will heal soon.'

Between them they loaded the still breathing Adey into the pastor's pride and joy.

'Now go, David – Devon – whoever you are. Don't come back here ever. Leave the car somewhere, I'll report it stolen tomorrow.'

'No!' Maeve shouted. She had been caught up in the quickly unfolding events, but one thought pushed forward in her mind. 'What about Elina? You left and now she's paying for all the things that you did with her.'

'With her, no.' Devon stopped and looked at her. 'She did nothing.'

'Then tell them. Go to the police and tell them,' pleaded Maeve. Devon sighed.

'I'm sorry, I can't do that. Just trust the system, she did nothing. It'll all be alright in the end.'

'But what if it's not?'

Devon looked at Maeve sadly. 'I'm sorry. Really.'

He turned away, got into the car, and drove away.

'Abigail,' said Maeve quietly. 'Is he really my dad?'

'Yes love, he is, and I'm your mum and I'll look after you.'

'I'm perfectly capable of looking after myself.' Maeve straightened 'You haven't been there for all this time, Elina has. You may be my mother, but she has always been my mum.'

'I know, and I've missed you every single day since you were taken.' Now that Abigail had found her daughter, she didn't want to lose her so soon. 'Come back inside and we'll talk over a cup of tea.'

They went in. Maeve sat down while Abigail busied herself making the tea. 'Just in a mug this time,' asked Maeve. 'I actually prefer it like that.'

Abigail chuckled, 'Okay, I usually do that when it's just me anyway.'

'How did Dad get here from the hospital? He was at death's door yesterday. What was in that test tube?'

Abigail sat down for a moment. 'Maeve, it's a long story, that's come to an end now. There are two tubes left, and they won't last very long. They are a very real miracle. They can give a person a new life. They are all that's left of Elliot.'

'Could they do the same for the pastor?'

'Yes,' said Abigail, 'But does he deserve it? You don't know what he was like.'

'Everyone deserves a second chance.'

'You're still young, aren't you? Life isn't just black and white.'

'How does it work though?' asked Maeve.

Abigail stood up and poured out the tea. 'Who knows? But it's something that's passed down through the family, and now Elliot's... That's it.'

'Isn't there anyone else in the family?'

'No, not like Elliot. And he's not having children is he?'

Maeve sat still.

Silent.

Thinking.

So long that Abigail wondered if she was alright.

'Abigail,' she said. 'About that, that business with Elliot. I haven't told anyone yet, but I think I'm pregnant!'

ABOUT THE AUTHOR

Brian J Twiddy was born in Kent, where success in a national young people's story competition sparked his interest. He has been an actor for many years, and following the establishing of Arty-Fact theatre company in 2001, with Yvonne Peacock, has written, a published series of 20 history playbooks, and 23 original plays and adaptations for young people. This is his first novel.

BRIANJTWIDDY.COM